THE THIEFTAKER

by
Darren Rapier

Darren Rapier

www.spannerintheworks.org.uk/tualen

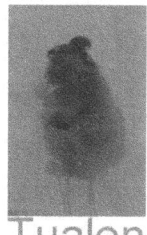

Tualen Press
PO Box 239
Sidcup
DA16 0DP
info@spannerintheworks.org.uk

First Published 2009

© Darren Rapier 2009
www.darrenrapier.co.uk

ISBN 978-0-9556798- 3-4

For a copy of the original songs email
info@darrenrapier.co.uk

For performance rights of this play please contact:

Andrew Mann Ltd.,
1 Old Compton Street,
London, W1D 5JA
Tel: 020 7734 4751
Fax: 020 7287 9264
info@andrewmann.co.uk

THE THIEFTAKER was first presented by
Full Scale Productions at Bridge Lane Theatre, Battersea,
Directed by Frances Moore
on 7th June 1994, with the following cast:

Counsel/ Jack Sheppard
Richard Waters

Gentleman/ Landlord/ Gaoler/ King George I/ John Gay/ Clerk
Drew Edwards

Jonathan Wild
Darren Rapier

Bailiff/ Toff-Smith/ Beadle/ Priest/
Pub Customer/ Friend at Hanging/ Henry
Richard Levesy

Fists/ Constable
Jason Brynford-Jones

Mary/ Mrs. Jackson/ Sheppard's Admirer
Alison Royce

Rouser/ Hitchin/ Benson/ Friend at Hanging/
Earl of Dartmouth/ James Thornhill/ Mr. Pargiter/ Field
Alistair Greener

Kneebone/ Blueskin/ Pub Customer/ Judge
Andy Leggatt

Bess/ Molly
Kate Eaton

Poll/ Mrs. Pargiter
Helen Verkerk

Darren Rapier

Notes on Setting and Style

(From the original production)

London, early 18th Century.

The action follows 'Epic' style.

'Projections' are separate from the scenes and merely state events, some of which may have a trickle down effect, although not immediately apparent. Dates are only normally relevant to the projection and not the scene.

Scenes are merely suggested by a few items of set and props. Titles of songs, captions etc., are to one side on an easel (like in Victorian Music Hall).

The scene descriptions may be flown in and out ie: 'A House in London'

Note also: JACK SHEPPARD's scenes are not chronological to WILD's until they meet.

Characters

Counsel – An 18th Century Barrister
Singer – A Ballad Singer
Gentleman – An 18th Century Dandy
Jonathan Wild – The first 'gangster' in London
Bailiff – A Representative of the Crown
Fists – A Bare Knuckle Fighter and Bruiser
Mary – A Prostitute and Wild's First Wife
Rouser – A Ringleader of the Mob
Toff – A Confidence Trickster
Smith – A Coin Forger
Kneebone – A Draper, Benefactor of Sheppard's
Jack Sheppard – The Famous Thief
Pub Customers/ Friends – 'Friends' of the Landlord
Landlord – An East End Publican
Bess – A Prostitute and Friend of Sheppard
Poll – A Prostitute and Friend of Sheppard
Hitchin – The Corrupt City Marshall
Henry – A Debtor
Thief – An innocent boy
King George I – The German Import Monarch
Woman Victim – An Elderly Victim of a Robbery
Mr. Pargiter – An Attourney
Mrs. Pargiter – The Attourney's Wife
Blueskin – A Violent Criminal
Molly – A Thief and Wild's Second Wife
Beadle – A Local Officer of the Law
Doorman – Servant of Wild
Benson – An Apprentice Thief
Constables – Parish Constables
Gaolers/ Guards – Slack and Crooked Thugs, Loyal to Wild
John Gay – The Writer
Pickpocket – Small time thief
Earl of Dartmouth – An Aristocrat with an Eye for a Bargain
Field – A Small Time Fence
James Thornhill – The Famous Artist
Ordinary – A Pious Fool
Woman at Gaol – An Admirer of Sheppard's
Clerk – A Clerk of Court
Mrs. Jackson - A Lacemaker
Judge – A Sage Old Fool
Jury – Various Gentlefolk

Darren Rapier

The Thieftaker
by
Darren Rapier

*A spotlight snaps on to the COUNSEL for the King: An
extremely well dressed early Eighteenth Century Lawyer.*

COUNSEL: Members of the jury I put it to you that for many
years past Mr. Jonathan Wild has been the
confederate with great numbers of highwaymen,
pick-pockets, housebreakers, shop-lifters and
other thieves.
That he has formed a kind of corporation of
thieves, of which he is head and director, and that
notwithstanding his pretended services, in
detecting and prosecuting offenders, he procures
such only to be hanged as conceal their booty, or
refuse to share it with him.
That he has divided the town and country into so
many districts, and appointed distinct gangs for
each, who regularly account with him of their
robberies.   That he has also a particular set to
steal at churches in time of divine service: and
likewise other moving detachments to attend at
court, on birth-days, balls etc. and at both houses
of parliament, circuits and country fairs.
That the persons employed by him are for the
most part felons convict, who have returned from
transportation before the time, for which they are
transported, is expired; and that he makes choice
of them to be his agents, because they cannot be
legal evidences against him, and because he has
it in his power to take from them what part of the
stolen goods he thinks fit, and otherwise use
them ill, or hang them as he pleases.
That he has from time to time supplied such
convicted felons with money and clothes, and
lodged them in his own house, the better to
conceal them: particularly some, against whom
there are now informations for counterfeiting and
diminishing broad pieces and guineas.

That he has not only been a receiver of stolen goods, as well as of writings of all kinds, for near fifteen years past, but has frequently been a confederate, and robbed along with the previously mentioned convicted felons.

That, in order to carry on these vile practices, to gain some credit with the ignorant multitude, he usually carries a short silver staff, as a badge of authority from the government, which he produces, when he himself is concerned with robbing.

That he has, under his care and direction, several warehouses for receiving and concealing stolen goods; and also a ship for carrying off jewels, watches, and other valuable goods, to Holland, where he has a superannuated thief for his factor.

That he keeps in pay several artists to make alterations, and transform watches, seals, snuff-boxes, rings and other valuable things, that they might not be known, several of which he used to present to such persons as he thought might be of service to him.

That he seldom or never helps the owners to the notes and papers they have lost, unless he finds them able exactly to specify and describe them, and then often insists on more than half the value.

And lastly, it appears that he has often sold human blood, by procuring false evidence to swear persons into facts they were not guilty of; sometimes to prevent them from being evidences against himself, and at other times for the sake of the great reward given by the government.

Projection: **In 1694 the City of London was made bankrupt by an Act of Parliament, because of overspending on rebuilding after the Great Fire. Privatisation of certain offices seemed an effective way to raise money. Offices including those of: Recorder; Keeper of Newgate and City Marshal were therefore auctioned off.**

Lights snap to 'song lighting'.   The BALLAD SINGER
steps forward.

BALLAD OF UNFULFILLMENT.

SINGER: Mr. Jonathan Wild,
When just a child,
One could tell he had Greatness in him.

Born Sixteen Eighty Two,
Not well to do,
Wolverhampton would be too small for him.

He gave it a try for a while,
Apprenticed and married like others,
Soon he had a child,
Some would be happy with that,
Not Mr. Wild.

Seventeen Oh Three,
Decided he,
Would desert and come to London.

Ran out on his wife,
For this new life,
The City received *all* with pleasure.

In London men lived like Kings:
Whoring or killing for Leisure,
Money was the thing,
That bought you happiness,
Or immunity.

What became of this man,
This Great man,
In the Greatest of Cities?

A Bucklemaker by trade,
The things he made,
Ornate, of value and beauty.

He moved to a grand house,

Darren Rapier

With servants and silver cutlery,
Free of his baby and spouse,
Surrounded in splendour,
But not his.

Lights snap to scene lighting.

Scene One: A House in London.

Caption: **1. Jonathan Wild looses his job.**

A GENTLEMAN stands before a mirror admiring his clothing.

GENT: Wild!   Where the devil are you?

WILD: Coming sir, just polishing the buckles you ordered.

Enter WILD with the buckles.

GENT: Ah, splendid, splendid.

WILD: The monogram on the left varies slightly from the right, but it's the best I could do with the time you gave me.

GENT: They look identical to me.   Is there a left and a right?

WILD: Well yes sir, I've rounded the outside corners slightly more.

GENT: Oh.   Excellent, excellent.   Like to see Thompson's face tomorrow at Mary-le-Bone Gardens, second pair of buckles in a fortnight, ha. (*He throws them into a small box, WILD seems annoyed at this*).   Now I'm off to St. James' for a spot of coffee, what do you think?

The GENTLEMAN turns to WILD, awaiting his comments on his attire.

WILD: Fine Sir.

GENT: Good.   Pass me my rings would you.

WILD fetches a small jewellery box and opens it, the GENTLEMAN takes out the rings and places them onto

Darren Rapier

his fingers. The GENTLEMAN freezes, Lights snap to
song lighting. WILD steps out of the action.

BALLAD OF ENVY.

WILD: Like magpies, with my eyes,
I see a glint.

Attracted, distracted,
I look, asquint.

He's my age, I'm enraged,
What right has he?

To have rings, and other things,
Instead of me!?

I don't have to stand for this,
I deserve much better,
If I had other's start in life,
I would not be a debtor,
Debtor, better
I deserve it more than you.

Given half a chance with looks and money I
could shine.
But undeserving bastards seem to have what's
rightly mine.

I don't have to stand for this,
I deserve much better,
If I had other's start in life,
I would not be a debtor,
Debtor, better
I deserve it more than you.

Deserve it more than you, so what am I to do?

Lights snap back to scene lighting.

GENT: Did you say something Wild?

WILD: No sir, looks fine sir.

GENT: Good, order me a chair would you.

WILD: Very well sir. (*He hesitates*).

GENT: Well?

WILD: I was... Wondering sir...

GENT: Yes, spit it out man.

WILD: The money you owe me sir, not for my wages, but the buckles sir. You see I've had to buy the silver, you know...

GENT: All in good time Wild, all in good time. You have no intention of leaving I take it.

WILD: Well no sir but...

GENT: Then there's no rush is there. I mean I'm not thinking of getting rid of you, at the moment.

WILD: Thank you sir.

GENT: Now run along and find me a sedan there's a good chap.

WILD: Yes sir.

WILD exits.

GENT: Give them an inch and they take a mile.

The GENTLEMAN returns to admiring himself in the mirror.
WILD returns.

WILD: Chair's waiting sir.

GENT: Very well. Blue coat today I think.

*WILD exits.   There is a knock at the door (off).
The BAILIFF enters.*

BAILIFF: Sorry to trouble you sir, it's Mr. Wild I'd like to
                speak to.

GENT: Oh, really.   Please feel free to use my house as a
                meeting place.

                *Enter WILD with the coat.   He acknowledges the
                BAILIFF but does not know him.*

GENT: I must say Wild this really is not on.

WILD: You said the blue one sir.

                *The BAILIFF steps forward and places his hand on
                WILD's shoulder.*

BAILIFF: I think he means me Jonathan.

WILD: ?

GENT: *(Putting on the coat).*   If you wish to rendezvous
                with your friends kindly do so in your own time.

BAILIFF: Oh I'm not a friend sir.   Jonathan Wild I am
                arresting you for bad debt to various persons
                within the City of London.

GENT: What!?

WILD: *(To BAILIFF).*   I'll get the money.   I'm owed it.

GENT: A debtor, in my service?

BAILIFF: Come on.

WILD: I'll pay it back!.

GENT: Look here Wild this just isn't on.   *(To BAILIFF)*
                How much does he owe the fellow?

BAILIFF: Fellow?

GENT: The Silversmith.

WILD: I couldn't let you pay sir.

GENT: Don't be absurd Wild, I have no intension of
paying. How much?

BAILIFF: The Silversmith? Ten pounds sir.

GENT: Ten pounds! *(To WILD)*. My God man! How
much did you expect for the buckles?

BAILIFF: Buckles?

WILD: I...

GENT: Never mind. Wild you've obviously no head for
money and I can only hope a short spell in the
Compter will put you straight.

WILD: But...

GENT: You can't expect things for nothing. You are
dismissed.

WILD: *(To audience)*. At which point I should give him
a piece of my mind but, things being what they
are, I can't afford to loose a potential future
employer. Besides further conversation may
lead to the discovery that there are twenty four
others, to whom I am indebted, so to speak.
Therefore I thank him and leave.

Exit WILD with the BAILIFF.

GENT: *(Calling off)*. Maria, check the cutlery would
you.

Exit the GENTLEMAN.

Darren Rapier

<u>**Projection:**</u>	**1707, the Parliamentary Act of 1697, to limit and regulate the number of 'Brokers' able to deal in stocks and shares, expired. Speculators could now trade unhindered. Within seven years the 'Bull' and 'Bear' were born.**

Scene Two: The Poultry Compter.

Caption: **2. A short spell of detention enables Wild to learn
more about crime.**

BALLAD OF THE VALUE OF EDUCATION.

> *The actors sing 'in character'.   Throughout the song a
> lone PRISONER sits in a corner of the stage, occasionally
> they may kick him.   He represents those wrongly
> imprisoned who do not wish to take up crime.   Throughout
> the song it is obvious that WILD is the favourite of
> MARY's 'admirers'.*

FISTS:
At school I barely learned to write,
Letters and numbers seemed like just a waste of
time,
At that age I also learned to fight,
Given the choice between a sign an' a fist,
Which would persuade and which might be
missed?

ALL:
The value of a good education,
Should not be devalued by mistrust,
Beware of academic qualifications,
In life a piece of paper's just not enough.

MARY:
When a man chases every girl he meets,
Pursuing a husband seems like just a waste of
time,
I've found that men pay for little treats,
Given the choice between a ring or the money,
Which pays the bills and which wears away?

ALL:
The value of a good education,
Should not be devalued by mistrust,
Beware of academic qualifications,
In life a piece of paper's just not enough.

ROUSER:
When younger I used to be ignored,
Shouting alone seemed like just a waste of time,
But people will listen to a mob,

Given the choice between reason or not,
Surely depends on the backing you've got?

ALL: The value of a good education,
Should not be devalued by mistrust,
Beware of academic qualifications,
In life a piece of paper's just not enough.

TOFF: I used to enjoy the masquerades,
But facade one evening seemed like just a waste
of time,
Better to use it every day,
Given the choice between a gent or a knave,
Of which are you wary, which expect to behave?

ALL: The value of a good education,
Should not be devalued by mistrust,
Beware of academic qualifications,
In life a piece of paper's just not enough.

SMITH: I worked hard for a year or two,
Grafting for hours seemed like just a waste of
time,
I decided to take what I was due,
Given the choice between paying or not,
Why shell out when you can nick the lot?

ALL: The value of a good education,
Should not be devalued by mistrust,
Beware of academic qualifications,
In life a piece of paper's just not enough.

As the others beat the PRISONER.

WILD: A short spot in the Poultry Compter,
Made my role in life much clearer,
Not much time just in and out,
Not much to pay by all accounts,
A life in crime now seems appealing,
This education's been revealing,
Contacts I've set up for good,
A ready made new livelihood,

Applying all the things I've learned,
A small misfortune seems upturned,

Given the choice between working or crime,
Which gets you rich in the shortest time?

ALL: The value of a good education,
Should not be devalued by mistrust,
Beware of academic qualifications,
In life a piece of paper's just not enough.

They file out singing with the body of the PRISONER.
Lights snap to song lighting and the BALLAD SINGER
steps forward.

BALLAD OF HONEST TOIL.

SINGER: The craft,
Of a man,
Or a woman,
Should not be,
Underestimated,
Denied,
Exploited,
Devalued,
Suppressed,
Crushed,
By anyone,
For anyone.

Scene Three: Mr. Kneebone's House in the Strand.

Caption: **3. Jack Sheppard fixes his benefactor's lock for free.**

SHEPPARD is sitting with a door lock in pieces on his lap. Enter KNEEBONE, well dressed.

KNEEBONE: Ah, Jack, just the person I wanted to see.

SHEPPARD: Nearly finished Mr. Kneebone.

KNEEBONE: Good, good. Now I wanted to have a word with you...

SHEPPARD: Mind if I finish this while we talk?

KNEEBONE: No, no, as you like. Erm, Jack you've been a great help to
me...

SHEPPARD: On the contrary Mr. Kneebone, you've helped me out no end. More than my father could ever have managed.

KNEEBONE: Yes.

SHEPPARD: Alright is he?

KNEEBONE: Yes, yes fine.

SHEPPARD: Don't seem to get enough time to get round and see him these days.

KNEEBONE: Ah, yes. Now...

SHEPPARD: Have you got your key?

KNEEBONE: Eh?

SHEPPARD: For the lock.

KNEEBONE: Oh, here you are.

SHEPPARD: Cheers. Better to use one.

KNEEBONE: Now Jack, it's very good of you to do these odd
jobs for me, but
I feel you've reached an age where you should
really be thinking about a career.

SHEPPARD: There. *(He demonstrates the lock, KNEEBONE
smiles).*

KNEEBONE: As I say a career...

SHEPPARD: What made you go into drapery?

KNEEBONE: Circumstance, the opportunity was there and I
took it. But, make no mistake, it's hard work
that has got me where I am today.

SHEPPARD: A good career move then?

KNEEBONE: Undoubtedly. Initially I wanted to be a lawyer
however, things being as they are, I was
obviously destined for other things.

SHEPPARD: You don't think you would have made it as a
lawyer then?

KNEEBONE: One likes to think one would 'make it' at
anything, but so few people succeed in executing
their ambitions I doubt if that can be the case.
We digress. A friend of mine, Owen Wood, has
a business further down the Strand, I expect
you've seen it on your way to the Chop House.

SHEPPARD: Carpenter's?

KNEEBONE: Yes. Now he is currently looking for a new
apprentice and, as you have some experience
from working with your father, I thought perhaps
you may be interested?

SHEPPARD: An apprenticeship?

KNEEBONE: As a carpenter, your father would be extremely pleased.

SHEPPARD: But my father's never had any money. He's been a carpenter all his life.

KNEEBONE: A noble profession Jack, fulfilment is far more important than financial gain.

SHEPPARD: Is it? *(To audience)* I can never decide.

KNEEBONE: Look I've provisionally told Owen that you will take the apprenticeship.

SHEPPARD: But, with all due respect Mr. Kneebone, that's seven years of my life.

KNEEBONE: Jack, seven years may seem a long time, but it will be over before you know it.

SHEPPARD: That's what I'm afraid of.

KNEEBONE: Jack it's not that long, I hated drapery when I started, some days I still do, but look what I've achieved with a little application.

SHEPPARD: It doesn't take seven years to learn how to shape a piece of wood.

KNEEBONE: Maybe it doesn't, but all apprenticeship are as long.

SHEPPARD: Why?

KNEEBONE: They just are: Seven seas, Seven sins, Seven Planets. No one questions why, it's just the way it is.

SHEPPARD: But...

KNEEBONE: Jack, this is good opportunity for you, I know you show aptitude in metal work and other areas

that constantly astound me, but people will
always need carpenters. Money isn't everything.
Besides I'm sure you will succeed in what ever
you do, I'll bet you five years from now the
whole of London will begging you to take their
money. I've told Owen you can start on
Monday, don't let me down.

Pause.

SHEPPARD: O.K.

KNEEBONE: Good, now get that lock on and I'll take you
down to the Swan for a celebratory drink.

*Exit SHEPPARD, followed by KNEEBONE with his arm
around JACK's shoulder.
Song lighting.*

BALLAD OF HONEST TOIL (reprise).

SINGER: The craft,
 Of a man,
 Or a woman,
 Should not be,
 Underestimated,
 Denied,
 Exploited,
 Devalued,
 Suppressed,
 Crushed,
 By anyone,
 For anyone.

Projection: **1708, the Government prohibited the issue of
monetary notes by an association of more
than six persons, effectively giving the Bank of
England (created by them to fund the
'revolutionary' idea of a 'National Debt') a
monopoly over their competitors.**

Scene Four: A House in Cripplegate.

Caption: **4.   Jonathan Wild buys a house with the money he's earned as Mary Milliner's pimp.**

Enter WILD (who now has a scar on his face) and MARY.

WILD: Well what do you think?

MARY: It's very nice.

WILD: Could you live here?

MARY: I could live anywhere, you know that.

WILD: Would you like to live here?

MARY: *(As if for the hundredth time).*   Who owns it?

WILD: *(Smiling).*   I do.

MARY: What?

WILD: I do.   What with the whoring money and a few little deals I've been doing on the side.

MARY: Our money?

WILD: Yeah, we had a price increase, well a few actually.

MARY: How come I didn't know about this?

WILD: Be serious Mary, you would have wanted a cut.

MARY: Bloody right I would have!

WILD: What was the point of telling you?   I thought it would be a nice surprise.

MARY: What would have been nice was a new pair of boots.

WILD: What's the point of that? It's not as if you spend much time on your feet is it? No you've got to be practical in this world: any man after a woman like you ain't going to be interested in the condition of her footwear, that's for sure.

MARY: I still think it's a bloody liberty.

WILD: Good management that's all; I managed to keep the extra without you finding out.

MARY: You pig.

WILD: I'm merely the butcher love. Anyway, there won't be any need for that any more.

MARY: Any what?

WILD: Selling your flesh. No, there's easier ways to make money. Consider yourself privatized, as of today your only requirement will be to keep me in the manner to which I will shortly become accustomed.

MARY: Give up prostitution?

WILD: A small price to ask.

MARY: But it's all I know.

WILD: Knew. Prostitution is a dead end game, it's time for a new start. You're not too old to retrain, put your talents to other uses. Besides I can't set up a legitimate business with a wife who makes a living for herself sleeping with other men.

MARY: It didn't bother you before... Wife?

WILD: Eh?

MARY: You said Wife.

WILD: To all intents and purposes.

MARY: What intents?

WILD: To the intent that I don't want you seen whoring. When I needed it fine, but that's finished now. *(He hands her some money).* Go out and get yourself some decent clothes, <u>decent</u>. From now on you're Mrs. Wild to anyone that matters, get it?

MARY: What if I choose not to join you in this 'exciting' new business venture.

WILD: Who said anything about choice? Sink or swim, *(Turns to audience).* And I'm not prone to using metaphors.

MARY: I could still make a living on my own you know, after all I'm the one with the goods.

WILD: No one wants to pay for damaged goods Mary. Now run along will you love.

MARY: It's my money too you know.

WILD: Trust me. I've managed to make the best use of it so far haven't I? This house is a monument to your hard work, but my business sense. We've used each other that's all, why break up a good business relationship?

   Pause

MARY: What sort of clothes shall I buy?

WILD: Something that says you belong to a very successful man.

   They smile at each other.

Projection: **In 1710 Saint Paul's Cathedral was finished. It had taken thirty five years to build.**

Originally Wren had drawn designs for rebuilding the whole city, with wide streets and magnificent quays, but thwarted by vested interests the scheme was never implemented.

Scene Five: The Black Lion, Drury Lane.

Caption: **5.   Jack Sheppard is taught a new craft.**

The LANDLORD is speaking with some FRIENDS.
SHEPPARD is trying to sell a wooden jewel box he has
made. Other CUSTOMERS sit around. EDGEWORTH
BESS and POLL MAGGOT are trying their luck with a
few of the men.

SHEPPARD: Come on gents a lovely jewel box for your
ladies, genuine velvet lining with a working
miniature lock.   Three levers, guaranteed a life
time.

CUSTOMER: Any jewellery in it?

SHEPPARD: I'm no goldsmith, I made the rest of it myself.

CUSTOMER: Couldn't afford it.

SHEPPARD: You don't know how much it is.

CUSTOMER: What's the point of a jewel box with no jewels?

SHEPPARD: It's to put your existing jewellery in.

CUSTOMER: Well they wear that don't they.

SHEPPARD: What about when she's not wearing it?

CUSTOMER: If she's not wearing it then she's got too much. No
if I got that, the next thing is she'll want me to fill
it, then I'll need a bigger box, then I'd fill that,
never ending.   I couldn't afford that, we've got
kids to feed, wasting our money on stones and
bits of metal.   Landlord!   Get us another two
jugs over here.

The LANDLORD comes over with the jugs.

LANDLORD: *(To CUSTOMER).*   Is he pestering you?

BESS: No, he's alright George.

The CUSTOMER pays for the drinks.

LANDLORD: Thanks. Like to know the time?

CUSTOMER: No.

LANDLORD: Free service, *(taking out his watch)* five to the hour.

CUSTOMER: That's a nice watch, you got there.

LANDLORD: Gold you know.

CUSTOMER: How'd you get that then?

LANDLORD: Never you mind. Let's say I acquired it. Keeps perfect time, unlike the rest of you.

SHEPPARD: Would you like a box?

LANDLORD: What sort of box?

SHEPPARD: To keep it in, seems a shame to scratch it.

LANDLORD: What do I want to keep it in a box for? I can afford to scratch it, solid gold see, not plated.

SHEPPARD: At night, surely you don't wear it in bed?

LANDLORD: Goes under my pillow, can't trust people round these parts.

SHEPPARD: That's O.K. put it in here and you won't hear it ticking all night.

The LANDLORD takes the box from him.

LANDLORD: It's well made, does the lock work?

SHEPPARD: Of course.

LANDLORD: All right then young man I'll take it.

SHEPPARD: Great.

LANDLORD: Beer or something to eat?

SHEPPARD: Beer please.

> *The LANDLORD goes and gets a beer. SHEPPARD looks pleased with himself, POLL and BESS watch with interest.*

LANDLORD: There we are young man.

SHEPPARD: Thanks. Right that'll be one guinea.

> *The pub is silent, all eyes on SHEPPARD.*

SHEPPARD: *(To audience).* Something told me this was not the way he normally did business.

LANDLORD: What?!

SHEPPARD: A guinea? Alright I'll knock a whole schilling off for the beer.

LANDLORD: I don't think you understand boy, that beer was a gift.

SHEPPARD: I need the money to pay my rent. It's a fair price. The watch must be worth six and thirty.

LANDLORD: That may be, but it cost me a beer, that makes your little box expensive enough I think, as much as a gold watch?

SHEPPARD: But I need the money.

LANDLORD: *(Throwing the box to the floor and taking the beer).* Then take it elsewhere!

BESS: *(To audience).* The true value of any item lies only on the current market price: That is what people are prepared to pay for a particular thing at a particular time. Workmanship, degradation or usefulness have no bearing on this.

JACK is picking up the broken box. BESS and POLL walk over to him.

SHEPPARD: It took me ages to get these corners right.

POLL: It's just a box Jack.

SHEPPARD: It is not just a box, it took me hours to finish.

BESS: So why spend so long on it?

SHEPPARD: Because I thought someone might appreciate the craftsmanship.

POLL: But it's still just a box Jack. I could spend all day making myself up, wouldn't make him want to pay any more for me. *(She gives the CUSTOMER a delicate wave and a smile, he waves back).*

BESS: She's right, if it does what people want it to, all they care about is the price.

POLL: Unless they can get more for their money. Then they like everyone to think they know how to get a good bargain.

BESS: Take George, he likes people to know he's got a thirty six guinea watch for a pint of beer, but only because it's worth more than he paid. He doesn't care how long the watch maker spent working out the diameter of the wheels and the number of teeth, or the wheel cutter tempering the metal, or the dial maker's enamelling. Let alone the goldsmith's and engravers time. All he cares about is that it tells the time and he got it cheap.

SHEPPARD: You're pretty sensible for a whore.

BESS: How many have you ever discussed social economics with?

POLL: You see Jack, all you've got to do is supply the right goods at the right price. No one cares about what you've had to go through, as long as the price is right.

SHEPPARD: But I still need to pay my rent Poll.

BESS: Look there's a friend of ours, Joseph Black, that's were George got his watch. Anyway he can get you a good price on most things, but he'll only do it as a favour. Forget the box, wait outside at about ten, when George goes out for his regular piss, swipe his watch.

SHEPPARD: But won't your friend recognise it?

POLL: He won't care he's had his beer, probably get about six guineas for it I reckon.

SHEPPARD: But it's worth over thirty.

BESS: But who ever buys it has to make a profit on it Jack, and still sell it for less than it's worth.

POLL: Who knows, you might find obtaining goods more profitable than making them, certainly easier. Blueskin, that's our friend, could do with a trainee, especially with you being so talented with locks. If you earned enough you could pack in your carpenter's apprenticeship.

SHEPPARD: People will always need carpenters.

BESS: But all they want is cheap carpenters Jack. If it's going to take you seven years how much are you going to charge for cutting a shelf to size? Think about it. If you want a coffee you don't go to

Mocha. How much of your schilling do you think those Arabs see? All they do is supply the product, it's the coffee houses that make the money. If all you want to do is earn a living, what difference does it make where the money comes from? Like Poll says, you've got a talent with locks why not use it for your benefit. No one will thank you for your effort or honesty, any more than you'll learn Arabic and write a letter of commendation.

SHEPPARD: But there's a difference.

BESS: If you get caught you'll probably only get your hand burned, it soon heals up, see.

POLL: It's supply and demand, same as us. If the demand wasn't there we wouldn't have to supply it. Besides it's not as if George didn't know that watch was nicked is it? Supply and demand.

BESS: See how you get on tonight, if no one wants to give you six guineas for the watch you can go back to your woodwork.

Projection: **1711, the South Sea Company was incorporated, and assigned a monopoly of British trade with Spanish America - The trade did not materialise.**

Scene Six: Greenwich, September 18th, 1714.

Caption: **6. While the crowds await the arrival of the new King, Jonathan Wild displays his commitment to justice and makes a valuable contact.**

The crowds (Including WILD, who from now on always wears a hat, MARY, FISTS, TOFF in fine gentleman's clothes etc. and CHARLES HITCHIN) await the arrival of George I.
The BALLAD SINGER sings for the crowd.

BALLAD OF PUBLIC SERVICE.

During which WILD notices the title, tuts and hands the BALLAD SINGER a piece of paper.

SINGER:　　　　When we're hungry and cold,
　　　　　　　The Saints of St.Pauls look on.

　　　　　　　When we're worked to death,
　　　　　　　The saints of St. Pauls look on.

　　　　　　　When we're stealing from each other,
　　　　　　　The saints of St.Pauls look on

　　　　　　　When we're killing each other,
　　　　　　　The Saints of St.Pauls look on.

　　　　　　　If they look on as we struggle here,
　　　　　　　Who cares that they'll outlast us all?
　　　　　　　The money allowed to Christopher Wren,
　　　　　　　Could have eased our present lives.

He looks at the paper WILD has handed him, he frowns. WILD gives him some money, he smiles. The music turns more upbeat...

SINGER:　　　　In times, when our property
　　　　　　　Remains our own for a very short time,
　　　　　　　And loss seems part of life, acceptable.

　　　　　　　When you can't, trust your fellow men,

- 34 -

All around screams and things disappearing
never seen.

Wouldn't you like to find help?
Wouldn't you like the chance of a small return?

For the mere fee of five schillings,
A new initiative,
Designed to beat the rise in crime.
At last opportunity,
To see precious things returned,
No question's asked, isn't it about time?

Have no fear your secrets will be safe,
The inquiry fee will guarantee,
The strictest privacy.

Mr. Jonathan Wild,
Will undertake the task,
Of bringing justice back,
To our broken City at last.

The crowd clap respectfully, WILD acknowledges.

HITCHIN: *(In London accent).*   Guten tag Herr Wild.

WILD: What?

MARY: Good day Mr. Hitchin.

HITCHIN: Ah, your wife speaks German? An intelligent
             lady, so useful to have another language.

WILD: She speaks French as well. In fact her
             intelligence is only surpassed by her sexual
             prowess, hence my admiration for the woman.

MARY forces a smile.
To one side of the stage a man (HENRY) tries to sneak
away without HITCHIN seeing him.

HITCHIN: Excuse me a moment would you.

Darren Rapier

HITCHIN walks briskly over to the man, who now has his back to him.

HITCHIN: This is a pleasant surprise Henry.

HENRY: Ah, Mr. Hitchin... I...

HITCHIN: How's the business going? *(Turning to audience)* A phrase with double meaning. The second being: You haven't paid your protection money, and shortly my friends will be paying you a visit to demonstrate both pain and suffering, in a short half hour session.

HENRY: It's been a bit quiet.

HITCHIN: Pity. However I'm sure things will liven up.

HENRY: It's the wife Mr. Hitchin, she's been poorly.

HITCHIN: Lucky you're able to run around for her, don't you think?

HENRY: Yes Mr. Hitchin.... I'll send the boy round to you in the morning.

HITCHIN: If it's a problem Henry, I'll always send someone over to you. You know that don't you?

HENRY: Yes Mr. Hitchin, thank you sir.

HITCHIN returns to WILD and MARY.

HITCHIN: As I was saying, I think it's important to learn a language.

WILD: Yeah, you should try English some time.

HITCHIN: You know what I mean Wild; the possibility of international communication, a true harmony of understanding, to the mutual benefit of the world as a whole.

WILD: Oh you've heard the King only speaks German as well then?

HITCHIN: I've... heard rumour that His Majesties preferred tongue is one of Germanic persuasion.

MARY: Germanic isolation was the impression I got.

HITCHIN: The man has simply been imported to fulfil a task, the least we can do as Englishmen is to show him some civility.

There is a commotion in the crowd, FISTS has hold of a man who is trying to escape his grasp. FISTS drags him over to WILD.

FISTS: Sorry John, I didn't realize you were talking to the City Marshal.

HITCHIN: Please, don't mind me.

WILD: What's the problem?

FISTS: This bloke's eyeing up some ladies purse, think he fancied a little fishing.

WILD: What with the King coming as well? Disgraceful.

THIEF: I didn't do nothing!

FISTS: Keep it closed or take it home in a bag.

MARY: *(To HITCHIN).* Is this your idea of a law abiding city?

HITCHIN: Madam I cannot control every individual.

WILD: He's right Mary, clearly there is a need for a support network: a private body that doesn't burden the tax payer with the problems of a small minority.

MARY: You mean like your own inquiry service Jonathan?

WILD: Yes dear. *(To HITCHIN)* Look, if Parliament saw fit to privatize your office what's the harm in a little sub-contracting? Improve your figures no end. You take care of your business and I'll take care of mine: specialize. You don't want to bother yourself with people asking you for things they've had nicked, you've got enough trouble making sure peoples livelihoods are protected.

HITCHIN: What exactly are you suggesting Wild?

WILD: Look, as City Marshal it's your job to keep order. Even in my line of business, inquiring after stolen goods, sometimes people need a little persuasion to co-operate. I'm just saying we could help each other out, that's all. Given a choice people will take a while to decide, take away that choice and it saves everyone a lot of time.

HITCHIN: And the bigger the organisation, the more it has to offer? The easier it is for the consumer.

WILD: Precisely. Why go elsewhere when everything you want is catered for under one roof?

HITCHIN: I like it. Come and talk to me so we can finalize the details.

WILD: Better still you come to me.

WILD hands him a leaflet.

HITCHIN: *(Looking at the THIEF).* What are you going to do with him?

WILD: I don't think you should encourage the petty
               thief, it creates a downward spiral. I'll sort it out.

WILD signals to FISTS, who takes the THIEF away.

HITCHIN: Box his ears and turf him out of the City?

WILD: Something like that.

HITCHIN: Probably Irish. Bloody foreigners left right and
               centre causing trouble. City's not our own any
               more. Let them in to do a simple job and the
               bastards don't want to leave.

CROWD: The King! *(They start waving).*

HITCHIN: Please excuse me Wild, official duties. You
               understand.

*WILD nods. HITCHIN pushes his was through the crowd
to greet King GEORGE. WILD and MARY exchange a
glance and smile. TOFF is shaking hands with the King
and HITCHIN bustles him aside.*

HITCHIN: Guten tag your Majesty.

GEORGE I: Ah, gut. Sie sprechen Deutch, ja? Wie geht es
               Ihnen? Es ist wunderbar die schöne Heimat
               sprache nocheinmal zu hören.

HITCHIN: Ah...

WILD: *(To audience).* Having someone else to blame
               makes it easier to neglect our own shortcomings;
               unless of course, like me, you haven't got any.

*Song lighting.
WILD walks to the Caption stand and reveals the next
one:*

Darren Rapier

BALLAD OF THE THIEFTAKER GENERAL OF GREAT BRITAIN AND IRELAND.

WILD: Who's name strikes fear into every villain in the City?
Who has information to fill the gallows every day?
Who shows no highwaymen nor pick purse any pity?
Who has the courts agreeing with every word they say?

ALL: The Thieftaker General.

WILD: That's me.

Armed with Prostitutes,
Highwaymen, Thieves, Pickpockets,
Burglars, former valets and footmen,
'Spruce Pigs' trained by a dancing master:
For court on Birth nights, balls, opera's and plays.

I divided London into districts,
Had separate specialized gangs in each.

Seven thousand Newgate Birds,
Under my control.

WILD begins to walk towards the audience.

So you, would come to me,
And ask me to find your stolen goods.
And I'd find them, charge you half the value,
And split your money,
With the very person who had robbed you.

If you're afraid I might pick on you,
Single you out from the audience...

Remember that fear!
Times one hundred it's what kept me going.

> Who's name strikes fear into every villain in the City?
> Who has information to fill the gallows every day?
> Who shows no highwaymen nor pick purse any pity?
> Who has the courts agreeing with every word they say?

ALL: The Thieftaker General.

WILD: That's me!

ALL: The Thieftaker General.

The lights snap to scene lighting.

Projection: **1714. Over the previous 75 years Britain had acquired a European reputation for political instability and judicial murder. Only Marlborough and Rooke's military victories had reversed this reputation for ineptitude and incompetence.**

Scene Seven: Wild's House in Cripplegate.

Caption: **7. Jonathan Wild makes mutually beneficial enquiries.**

> *The LANDLORD of the Black Lion sits at WILD's desk, WILD joins him, FISTS stands guard and SMITH sits in the background with a ledger.*

LANDLORD: ...So you see Mr. Wild it has great sentimental value to me.

WILD: Yet the monogram doesn't match your initials?

LANDLORD: A family nickname.

WILD: I see. *(Pause)* Give your five shillings to my colleague and we'll see what we can do.

LANDLORD: Err, five shillings?

WILD: Enquiry money.

LANDLORD: I have a pub in Drury Lane, perhaps you would like to pop over for a drink and something to eat sometime?

WILD: It's still five shillings. A small price for such a 'sentimental object'.

> *THE LANDLORD hands the money to SMITH, who writes it into a little book and gives him a receipt.*

LANDLORD: What if you don't find the watch?

WILD: The enquiry would have still been made. Call back in a week.

> *The LANDLORD starts to ask another question but a look from FISTS tells him this would not be wise. The LANDLORD exits.*

WILD: Has that watch been broken up yet?

SMITH: *(Producing a second book)* No, but it was due
                to go to Holland this week with the other scrap.

WILD: O.K. get it back. *(Pause).* Where did it come
                from?

SMITH: Blueskin.

WILD: And yet the Landlord reckons it was swiped?
                (Beat) Pick-pocketing ain't Joseph Black's game
                any more; for a lousy gold watch? Put the word
                out Fists, I'd like a little chat with our friend
                Blueskin.

> There is a knock at the door. FISTS opens it and a
> WOMAN enters, she has a bruised face and seems
> distraught. WILD helps her to a seat.

WOMAN: Thank you.

WILD: Smith, a glass of gin for the lady.

WOMAN: This is the Thieftaker General's?

WILD: You're speaking to him madam, 'Over thirty
                criminals brought to the gallows'.

WOMAN: I had hoped I should never need your services
                Mr. Wild, but as you can see I have been the
                victim of a cruel and vicious crime.

> SMITH hands her the gin.

WOMAN: Thank you. Yesterday I returned to my home in
                Henrietta Street to find a man helping himself to
                my belongings. When I challenged him, he
                knocked me to the ground and demanded I tell
                him the whereabouts of my valuables.

WILD: Have you been to the authorities madam?

WOMAN: They were less than sympathetic.

WILD: Usually the case I'm afraid.   In fact they come to
            me for help these days.

WOMAN: So I'd heard.

WILD: Do you have a list of what was taken?

WOMAN: Certainly, here.

> WILD studies the list, he seems surprised by a couple of
> items.

WILD: Tell me, would you be able to describe this man?

WOMAN: Why, yes.   He was...

WILD: Probably best not to.   Just confuse the issue,
            masters of disguise you see, some of these
            villains.

WOMAN: But don't you want even a rough idea, how can
            you be sure you will be looking for the right
            man?

WILD: Oh don't worry about that.   I haven't got my
            reputation as 'The Thieftaker General' for
            nothing.

SMITH: *(To audience)*   Although the title was his own
            idea.

WILD: Take my word for it, the man you see in court
            will be hanged for this crime.

WOMAN: That's good enough for me.

WILD: Now, if you'd give your five shillings to Mr.
            Smith we can start our enquiries right away.   I'm
            sorry to ask you this, but even the authorities pay.

WOMAN: I understand, we can't expect things for nothing in this world.

She hands the money to SMITH who gives her a receipt.

WILD: Within a week I'll have someone in the dock at the Old Bailey.

WOMAN: I shall look forward to testifying against him.

FISTS opens the door for her and the WOMAN exits.

WILD: Some people simply don't how to behave. Who robbed that house in Henrietta Street?

SMITH: Rouser.

WILD: That good for nothing toerag. *(He looks at the WOMAN's list).* Silver snuff box, one gold heart locket and a miniature. We seem to have every thing else. Thought he'd slip one over on us didn't he?

FISTS: Do you want him brought in?

WILD: No, not yet. *(To audience)* Oh the children are playing up again. Smith, what did we do with that idiot we picked up at Greenwich?

SMITH: He's still in the Poultry Compter.

WILD: Right, we'll fit him up for this, the old bag'll be pleased to see anyone swinging for it. He's not worth more than the forty quid reward, *(Looks at FISTS)* not even a proper villain. *(Beat)* Right, I'm off to string a few up at Tyburn, blue coat today I think.

FISTS hands him the coat.

WILD: *(As he leaves).* My children are coming.

Darren Rapier

FISTS and SMITH look at each other.

<u>**Scene Eight:**</u> Hampstead Heath.

<u>Caption:</u> **8. Jack Sheppard and Joseph Black (Alias Blueskin) have joined forces and enjoy regularly robbing with violence.**

PARGITER and his WIFE are making their way across the bleak heath.

WIFE: …I still say that we should have waited for a carriage.

PARGITER: It really isn't that far to walk.

WIFE: But what if something happens?

PARGITER: A man should be able to walk were he likes, when he likes, this isn't the dark ages for goodness sake.

WIFE: But it's not safe.

PARGITER: Look, if anyone approaches us just give them what we have, it's not as if we're loaded with the crown jewels.   Nothing that we have is worth risking ourselves for, remember that.

WIFE: But what if they don't ask, or we don't realize they want our things?

PARGITER: Look, I've read about this.   I deal with criminal law.   At the command of 'Stand and Deliver' we simply hand over our money and they will leave us alone.   They are reasonable men after all.

WIFE: Let's go back.

PARGITER: How many more times, there's nothing to worry about.

> *SHEPPARD and BLUESKIN jump on him.   They beat him until he collapses. PARGITER's WIFE screams. SHEPPARD grabs her around the mouth.*

PARGITER: You didn't say stand and deliver.

> *BLUESKIN kicks him.   He takes his watch and his wedding ring, he pulls off his coat.   BLUESKIN admires the cut of the cloth.*

BLUESKIN: What's your trade?

PARGITER: Attorney.

BLUESKIN: You should brush up on your defence my friend. Purse.

> *PARGITER hands him the purse.   BLUESKIN walks towards his WIFE.   SHEPPARD spins her round and pushes her into BLUESKIN who restrains her.*

PARGITER: She hasn't got anything!

> *SHEPPARD pulls PARGITER to his feet and hits him repeatedly until he collapses.   Slowly he walks over to his WIFE, she tries to struggle away but BLUESKIN holds her.   SHEPPARD takes her hand, holding it firmly he gently removes the rings.   She pulls her hand away. SHEPPARD takes the other hand and repeats the procedure.   He looks at her neck, he snatches a pendant from it.*

SHEPPARD: Now, is there anything else?

> *PARGITER's WIFE shakes her head.   SHEPPARD approaches her.   He smiles and then forcefully kisses her.*

SHEPPARD: Then we'll have to take your word for it.

> *BLUESKIN throws her to the floor, she rushes over to PARGITER.*

BLUESKIN: We are gentlemen after all. *(He takes a shilling out of the purse and throws it onto the floor).* For a carriage home, you don't know who you might bump into round here?

SHEPPARD tips his hat, he and BLUESKIN smile and exit. PARGITER's WIFE is left tending to her husband on the ground.

Scene Nine: Wild's House in Cripplegate.

Caption: **9. Wild asserts authority over his empire.**

> *The stolen items from PARGITER are lying on the table.*
> *SHEPPARD stands, WILD and BLUESKIN are seated.*
> *FISTS stands at the door, SMITH seated in the corner.*

SHEPPARD: …Yet it's worth twice as much.

WILD: I can only ask the owner for half their value, if he ever turns up. If not I'll be lucky to get that. I'm the one taking the risk here, think yourself lucky you're with Mr. Black.

> *SHEPPARD turns sharply to shout at WILD. He catches*
> *BLUESKIN's eye and is warned against it.*

BLUESKIN: It's a fair price Jonathan. The lad's new to it that's all, still thinks in retail.

> *WILD nods. He stands and indicates his chair to*
> *SHEPPARD.*

WILD: Sit down.

> *After a short pause SHEPPARD sits. WILD picks up a*
> *silver staff with a crown at the head. He taps the head*
> *into his palm a few times.*

WILD: Did you know that the mace was the preferred weapon of the clergy during the crusades? One swift blow from horseback could crush a man's skull. No need to worry about accusations of bloodshed, most of the bleeding was internal. The day's of chivalry eh, you knew who you could trust then? People knew their place. *(He turns to face BLUESKIN).* Which reminds me Joseph, since when have you been demoted to a pickpurse?

BLUESKIN: What?

WILD: Gold watch.

BLUESKIN: Oh that. Merely helping out a friend Mr. Wild.

WILD: Nothing wrong with helping a friend. You see
                 the thing is Mr. Jack Sheppard every villain in
                 London has a friend: A person who will buy his
                 booty. Without that friend the thief cannot exist.
                 Prime beef is simply a slaughtered carcass when
                 no one wants to eat meat. There are only two
                 types of villain in London: those who deal with
                 me and those I deal with; bad children end their
                 days on the gallows Mr. Sheppard.

Snap to song lighting.

BALLAD OF RETRIBUTION.

BALLAD SINGER steps forward.

SINGER: Don't think you've got away,
                 Just because nothing's happened today,
                 You'll be caught out,
                 No doubt about-
                 That,
                 Is there?

                 Good deeds don't go unnoticed,
                 Help others you'll be rewarded,
                 Won't you?

                 See it in life,
                 Don't you?

                 Don't you?

Scene Ten: Newgate Gaol.

Caption: **10. Jonathan Wild severs his friendship with former City Marshal Charles Hitchin.**

HITCHIN is in the condemned hole behind bars. WILD enters, pays the GAOLER (who exits) then stands outside the cell with FISTS (both well dressed).

HITCHIN: Wild. Thank God.

WILD: Just visiting a few friends, thought I'd pop in.

HITCHIN: I'm out of money, they gave my Tuesday loaf to the debtors because they had a few visitors.

WILD: I've ordered us some wine.

HITCHIN: I knew you wouldn't let me down.

Enter the GAOLER with wine and cups. He places them next to WILD and exits. FISTS pours out three cups and hands them out.

WILD: To justice.

WILD and FISTS raise their glasses, HITCHIN does so begrudgingly.

HITCHIN: How's your good lady?

WILD: I have another.

HITCHIN: Oh?

WILD: What with business being so good, I've moved up market. Naturally I've seen Mary alright, she's a good girl, but not cut out for the upper echelons of society.

HITCHIN: Good to see you're still successful.

WILD: Cornered the market Charles. Just moving to bigger premises actually, nice place, opposite the Old Bailey.

HITCHIN spits out his wine in surprise.

WILD: Well it's easier for me, when I'm conducting the old prosecutions, you know. Shame you won't see it.

HITCHIN: Oh don't worry about that, I haven't got any fear of that place. Take more than the Old Bailey to keep me from visiting an old mate.

WILD: You planning on getting out then Charlie?

HITCHIN: Well, yes.

WILD: Really? Blackmail and extortion? You must have friends in pretty high places mate. *(To audience)* Watch his face, picture.

HITCHIN's face drops.

HITCHIN: But...

WILD: Something the matter Charles? Wine alright? Should be it's the best in the house, no one in Newgate would dare put one over on me.

HITCHIN: You've got to get me out of here.

WILD: Me? The Thieftaker General of Great Britain and Ireland, help a lowly criminal like you?

WILD looks at FISTS and they laugh falsely.

HITCHIN: I can't stand this.

WILD: You won't have to much longer, their hanging you next week.

HITCHIN: Get me out of here Wild.

WILD: Charles. Charlie. There is nothing I like better than helping a friend, you know that, but what you have done is despicable. You have been entrusted with upholding the law, and you've betrayed that trust. I can't be seen associating with lowlife filth, what would my public say?

HITCHIN: Jonathan I'll do anything, work as a footpad, anything, just get me out.

WILD: You don't understand do you? You are a marked man, soiled goods. No use to me. I'll get you some food in, few bottles of wine, but that's all I can do. I'm not a God Charlie, no matter what people say. So long.

WILD signals to FISTS, who opens the door, they exit leaving the wine.

HITCHIN: Wild! Wild! Help me!

Projection: **The Jacobite rebellion in Scotland, led Parliament to pass the Riot Act. £100,000 reward was offered for the capture of 'the Pretender' James Stuart.**

Scene Eleven: Wild's office, near the Old Bailey.

Caption: **11.**   **Jonathan Wild uses his power to help a friend in need.**

PARGITER sits at the table, his stolen goods laid out before him. WILD is standing, FISTS at the door and SMITH in the corner.

WILD: Mr. Pargiter are these the goods you had stolen or not?

PARGITER: Yes as I say, I merely would like to know how you obtained them?

WILD: Do you want them back?

PARGITER: At least a description of the men.

WILD: I run a large organisation, keeping tabs on where each item comes from would be impossible.

PARGITER: They all came from one source though?

WILD: I really couldn't say.

PARGITER: Couldn't or wouldn't?

WILD: Mr. Pargiter, you knew the deal when you paid your five shillings: 'no questions asked'. You have entrusted me to find your belongings, I've kept my part of the bargain.

PARGITER: That may be Mr. Wild, but I was the victim of an unprovoked and vicious attack.

WILD: So is half of London!   It's part of life, most people just accept it, they're grateful they can get something back.

PARGITER: Please forgive me for not asking you to thank my attackers.

WILD: If you want it it's half the value, I simply offer a
                    paid service. *(To audience)* This bloke's
                    giving me grief because he's been the victim of a
                    crime. Imagine if I was one of those new
                    insurance companies, asking for money before
                    he'd even been robbed. Some people?

PARGITER: I seem to have no choice.

*SMITH steps forward to take the money and write a
receipt.*

SMITH: There's always a choice sir.

*There is a knock at the door. MOLLY enters holding a
bundle containing stolen goods.*

WILD: *(Loudly for PARGITER's benefit).* Oh, it's the
                    wife. Back from the grocer's so soon love?

MOLLY is puzzled, but then sees PARGITER.

MOLLY: Yes.

WILD: Mr. Pargiter's an attorney. Him and his lady
                    wife were accosted on Hampstead Heath.

MOLLY: Oh, it's terrible up there isn't it?

PARGITER: Have you ever been attacked there then Mrs.
                    Wild?

MOLLY: No, but me and Jonathan seem lucky that way,
                    with what you hear and everything.

PARGITER: Yes.

WILD: Good day Mr. Pargiter, I'm sure your wife's
                    missing you.

PARGITER: She daren't step out of the house.

WILD: She'll get over it.

PARGITER is ushered out by WILD and then FISTS.
WILD gives a gentle wave as the door is shut, before
turning venomously to Mary..

WILD: What do you want to go bringing those back in
here for you silly cow!? They're for export.

MOLLY: I know.   Jonson's been taken.

WILD: What?

MOLLY: The authorities have captured our sloop and
Captain Jonson with it.

WILD: Where is he now?

MOLLY: The Riverside Watch House.

WILD: Damn, just when we need him.   Much on board?

MOLLY: Full.

WILD: He's for the gallows then. *(Beat)*   Smith.

SMITH: Yep.

WILD: Get Rouser, tell him to take some of his boys
down to the Riverside Watch and create a
disturbance.   I'll get some Dubbers together to
crack him out.   Sort out a safe house as well
would you, he's too valuable to lose.

Exit SMITH via the back.

MOLLY: What shall I do with this stuff?

WILD: I'll take it over to the Garden, get it re-shaped and
back on the market by morning.   No one,
especially the authorities gets one over on
Jonathan Wild.

MOLLY: Don't forget they're hanging Hitchin tomorrow.

WILD: Oh yeah. I wanted to see that as well. I'll see if
      I can get it delayed until the afternoon.

He kisses MOLLY on the cheek.

WILD: See you later, don't wait up.

Exit WILD and FISTS.

Scene Twelve: St. Giles's Roundhouse.

Caption: **12. Sheppard rescues Edgeworth Bess from the Roundhouse.**

A tableau: BESS distressed behind bars, the evil BEADLE standing on the other side. The actor playing SHEPPARD speaks directly to the audience.

SHEPPARD: Let it not be said that Jack Sheppard doesn't know anything about decency and loyalty. Edgeworth Bess, to whom he owes his start on the road to notoriety, lies imprisoned in Saint Giles's Roundhouse.   He could leave her there? After all there is no shortage of women eager to take her place, but no - He visits the Roundhouse…

SHEPPARD enters the tableaux, it is re-created. SHEPPARD shakes the BEADLES hand, BESS reaches through the bars for her champion. SHEPPARD turns to the audience.

SHEPPARD: Chats to the BEADLE for a while.

Tableau re-created, BESS watches as SHEPPARD places his arm around the BEADLE and they are laughing.

SHEPPARD: Gaining his confidence, Sheppard hits him over the head.

Tableau re-created, the BEADLE falling to the floor as a gleeful SHEPPARD hits him. BESS claps with excitement.

SHEPPARD: Taking his keys, Sheppard frees Bess.

Tableau re-created, SHEPPARD opening the door and BESS rushing out to greet him. The BEADLE lies on the floor.

SHEPPARD: They leave for a celebratory drink.

Tableau re-created, BESS and SHEPPARD leaving arm in arm, stepping over the BEADLE. SHEPPARD steps out of the tableaux, BESS exits, the BEADLE's body still lies uncomncious.

SHEPPARD: Now, if that isn't an act of decency what is?

Projection: **1718. In light of certain practices it became a felony to accept money for the return of stolen goods: unless information about the supplier of such goods was given. 'Handling' stolen goods became a criminal offence for the first time.**

Scene Thirteen: Wild's house near the Old Bailey.

Caption: **13. Jonathan Wild embraces the principals of the new law.**

WILD and MOLLY are enjoying a five course meal with guests: FISTS, SMITH, ROUSER and TOFF among others. Servants attend them, WILD is reading a paper. Conversations cross subjects.

WILD: See our Mr. Sheppard's getting quite a name for himself.   He's escaped from Saint Giles's now.

MOLLY: Popular with the ladies.   Quite the gentleman I've heard.

FISTS: Bit of a bruiser by all accounts.

WILD: That'll be Blueskin's influence, I worry about that man.

MOLLY: He broke into the Roundhouse previously, just to set one of his girlfriends free.

ROUSER: Sheppard ain't that tough, get him on his own.

SMITH: Most people hand over the cash at the mention of his name now.

MOLLY: Would you do that for me Jonathan?

TOFF: Reputation you see, counts for everything.

WILD: Wouldn't have to love.

ROUSER: Do you want him taken out?

SMITH: He gets some good stuff.

MOLLY: Be a shame to see him go, always got a smile.

TOFF: Not in your league Jonathan.

WILD: See what the reward goes to.

ROUSER: See how cocky he gets.

WILD: Yeah. More wine?

ROUSER: Don't mind if I do.

Enter a DOORMAN.

DOORMAN: A Mr. Pargiter to see you sir.

WILD: Oh what does he want now?

SMITH: Hasn't been turned over.

WILD: Alright I'll be out in a minute.

The DOORMAN exits.   WILD and FISTS stand.

WILD: Finish your meal boys.   Rouser, take what's left
               with Molly down to Jack Ketch's warren. *(To
               audience)* I may be rich, but it can't be said I
               don't help out those less fortunate than myself.

*WILD and FISTS walk through to the office where
PARGITER awaits.*

WILD: Mr. Pargiter, what a pleasant surprise.

PARGITER: I'll get straight to the point Wild, your days are
               numbered.   Have you seen the papers today?

WILD: Browsed through them.

PARGITER: Obviously missed the article to which I allude, or
               the sort of papers you read don't cover such
               things.

WILD: 'Devil worshipper Duncan (34), wins lottery with
               666'?

PARGITER: Very amusing, but I refer to the law.

WILD: And they refer to me.

PARGITER: I am afraid Mr. Wild that your business practices have caused a great deal of concern, to certain members of the establishment.

WILD: I'm not surprised: people have a habit of noticing things when others start to make money, probably upset they're not getting a cut. But there's really no need to be afraid Mr. Pargiter, is there?

PARGITER: You can't threaten me Wild.

WILD: I don't threaten people, I don't need to. I run a respectable business.

There is a knock at the door. FISTS opens it and the LANDLORD from the Black Lion enters.

LANDLORD: Oh, sorry Mr. Wild, I'll call back.

WILD: Not at all, please come in.

LANDLORD: It's about my watch...

WILD: Stolen again?

LANDLORD: Yeah, it's not worth owning anything decent in this world.

WILD: Well, I'm sure we'll find it for you.

LANDLORD: At this rate I might as well have bought a new one... *(He realises what he has said).* If it hadn't been in the family already I mean.

The LANDLORD goes to hand WILD five shillings.

WILD: Please, put your money away.   My enquiry
                  service is free now, it may not turn up after all;
                  things are harder to come by now that villains
                  know I'm at liberty to turn them in.   Still, if it
                  makes London a safer place to live I'm all for it.
                  Don't you agree Mr. Pargiter?

            PARGITER storms out.

WILD: Can't please everyone.   *(Turns to LANDLORD).*
                  You've caught me in a generous mood.   Send
                  one of your barmaids to Turnagain Lane at
                  eleven, with nine guineas: You'll have your
                  watch.

LANDLORD: A quarter, but...

WILD: No questions asked.

            The LANDLORD nods gratefully and exits.

WILD: Fists, put an add in the Post: 'Due to public
                  demand The Thieftaker General's enquiry service
                  will continue, free of charge'.

Projection: **1719, The South Sea Company approached
                  the government with a speculative scheme to
                  absorb the National debt of £30,000,000.   The
                  Bank of England tried to compete as they
                  were nervous of this financial rival.**

Scene Fourteen: Leicester Fields.

Caption: **14. Jack Sheppard is wrongly accused and arrested.**

Leicester Fields are full of people talking of buying and selling shares in companies. SHEPPARD and a friend BENSON, as well as the LANDLORD, are present. The scene is frozen as SHEPPARD sings.

SHEPPARD: What are we to do with undesirables?
Sweep them under the carpet?
Don't acknowledge their existence,
It will encourage others.

Get them off the streets?
We don't want to see them.
Don't write about them,
(Well just a little),
Merely to show how bad they are.

We don't need to teach them,
Show them alternatives,
Just a harsh sharp shock,
They won't want to do it again.

Lock me up it's a welcome break,
When I decide I'll be back again.
If a prison must be so harsh and cruel,
A survivor must be invincible.

If a prison must be so harsh and cruel,
A survivor must be invincible.

Scene lighting.

BENSON: So then what?

SHEPPARD: Out, over the tiles, into the churchyard and away.
Didn't realize I'd gone 'till the next morning.

BENSON: What if they'd caught you?

SHEPPARD: Nothing to lose. Hanging, or transportation either way. You have to ask yourself: What can be achieved by my sitting here and letting life walk all over me? If you see an opportunity take it, it's how society works. *(To audience)* That's the one I'm not fit for by the way.

BENSON: It doesn't work like that though. I took a chance: made an investment the other day, put me in debt. Definite earner as well: bloke had this devise for extracting silver from lead.

SHEPPARD: Did it work?

BENSON: Turns out some french bloke's nicked the design and started using it over there first. He was livid. I gave him everything I had and apparently he'd invested four times that, of his own money, poor sod.

SHEPPARD: Why bother with lead when there's plenty of silver around, or gold for that matter. Do you think Sir Francis Drake studied mining? No, he took what he wanted once other people had done all the work. Apparently even Shakespeare stole a lot of his stuff. All noble men. We're merely picked on because we have the misfortune of lowly parentage.

BENSON: Prison hasn't deterred you then?

SHEPPARD: Far from it, things haven't changed out here have they?

They walk behind the LANDLORD who is talking to some friends. He is showing them his hand, filled with rings.

LANDLORD: ...course that's not what they cost me, what with me owning a stake in the company, gold and stones are dirt cheap out there. Stock's gone up again today I see.

BALLAD OF ENVY (reprise).

BENSON: Like magpies, with my eyes,
I see a glint.

Attracted, distracted,
I look, asquint.

Twice my age, I'm enraged,
What right has he?

To have rings, and other things,
Instead of me!?

I don't have to stand for this,
I deserve much better,
If I had other's start in life,
I would not be a debtor,
Debtor, better
I deserve it more than you.

BENSON taps the LANDLORD on the shoulder and speaks over the music.

BENSON: Excuse me do you have the time?

The LANDLORD turns and, (in animated silence) as the song continues, tells BENSON the exact time and the fact his watch is accurate and gold etc.

A gold watch, looks topnotch,
Solid gold chain.

Quite flashy, unlike me,
I'm not that vain.

He thinks he's, the bees knees,
Dressed to kill.

Hasn't the, right manner,
To fit the bill.

I don't have to stand for this,
I deserve much better,
If I had other's start in life,
I would not be a debtor,
Debtor, better
I deserve it more than you.

Given half a chance with looks and money I
could shine.
But undeserving bastards seem to have what's
rightly mine.

I don't have to stand for this,
I deserve much better,
If I had other's start in life,
I would not be a debtor,
Debtor, better
I deserve it more than you.

Deserve it more than you, so what am I to do?

*BENSON goes to grab the watch but the LANDLORD,
prepared for such events, has another long chain
attached. To shouts of 'Thief!' etc. he pulls the watch
from BENSON's hand as he runs off. SHEPPARD stands
dumbstruck. Realising attention has switched to him he
goes to run but is held by a few of the LANDLORD's
FRIEND's.*

LANDLORD: I know you.

SHEPPARD: I ain't interested in your poxy watch!

FRIEND: That's Jack Sheppard.

A Parish CONSTABLE arrives.

CONSTABLE: Something the matter gentlemen?

LANDLORD: Is there a reward for the capture of Jack
              Sheppard?

CONSTABLE: Probably.

LANDLORD: *(Indicating SHEPPARD).* This man tried to take
my watch. Would you like my name and
address?

Scene Fifteen: Newgate Gaol.

Caption: **15. With the help of Edgeworth Bess and Blueskin, Jack Sheppard escapes from Newgate.**

The BALLAD SINGER steps forward.

BALLAD OF LOYALTY.

SINGER: Let me tell you of loyalty,
Unsurpassed in this tale,
Of the woman who helped the man,
And wound up in Gaol.

She came as a visitor,
But was taken for a wife,
Committed to her lovers cell,
To pay with her life.

So take note you candidates,
With your promises full flow,
If you showed us such loyalty,
Perhaps we'd follow.

SHEPPARD and BESS are in the cell, a GUARD sits outside. BLUESKIN enters.

BLUESKIN: Well, well, fancy finding you here.

BLUESKIN holds out his hand as if to shake SHEPPARD's. SHEPPARD returns the gesture and palms a file from BLUESKIN.   He hands it behind him to BESS, who conceals it.

SHEPPARD: Just a social visit Joseph?

BLUESKIN: Yes, normally I'd stay but you know how it is? Nice room Jack.

SHEPPARD: Strongest in the Newgate Ward apparently.

BESS: Nice view.

BLUESKIN: Mr. Wild been in?

SHEPPARD: Not to see me.

BLUESKIN: Well, looks like you're for it then. Better have a last drink together.

BLUESKIN turns to the GUARD.

BLUESKIN: You wouldn't mind helping me choose a good year would you?

GUARD: I don't get paid to recommend the claret you know?

BLUESKIN drops some money into his hands.

GUARD: However I am known for my excellent advice, as regards liquid refreshment.

BLUESKIN and the GUARD exit to another room, the GUARD shows BLUESKIN's various bottles as:

SHEPPARD: *(To audience)* You don't want to sit there while I file through four iron bars do you? Right, suffice as to say, the deed is done.

SHEPPARD and BESS tie the bed sheets together and make a rope. They climb out of the window and escape as:

BLUESKIN: Surely you can't tell by looking at the bottle? Money is no object. Unfortunately I have an allergic reaction to drink, it makes me fall over, so if you wouldn't mind.

GUARD: I am on duty Mr...?

BLUESKIN: Like I said money is no object.

GUARD: *(With mock reluctance).* If you insist.

The GUARD tastes the wine as if a connoisseur. He shakes his head, needing another glass.

BLUESKIN: Well?

GUARD: This'll do.

BLUESKIN: Would you mind just finishing that bottle, make sure the sediment tastes alright.

GUARD: If you insist.

The GUARD downs the rest of the bottle in one, he staggers back as the effect hits him. He is drunk, BLUESKIN smiles at him, the GUARD chuckles, BLUESKIN laughs with him (falsely). BLUESKIN takes a quick look into the cell. The GUARD is still laughing.

BLUESKIN: Oh, I've just remembered, I've got an urgent engagement. Take that in for me would you.

Still laughing the GUARD takes the bottle and a few cups. BLUESKIN pats him on the back and exits. The GUARD enters the room with the cell, he looks round, his laugh peters out.

GUARD: Bollocks.

Projection: **Everyone wanted to own shares in new companies and invest in speculation, new inventions were abound. The South Sea Company became eager to stamp out it's small rivals.**

Scene Sixteen: Hatton Garden.

Caption: **16. Sheppard and Blueskin decide to go against Jonathan Wild.**

There is a sign in the background, with an arrow pointing off stage saying "GOLD, SILVER AND OTHER STOLEN ITEMS BOUGHT, BEST PRICES, NO QUESTIONS ASKED."

BALLAD OF INVINCIBILITY (reprise).

SHEPPARD/	
BLUESKIN:	What are we to do with undesirables?
	Sweep them under the carpet?
	Don't acknowledge their existence,
	It will encourage others.
	Get them off the streets?
	We don't want to see them.
	Don't write about them,
BLUESKIN:	(Well just a little),
SHEPPARD:	Merely to show how bad they are.
BLUESKIN:	We don't need to teach them,
SHEPPARD:	Show them alternatives,
BLUESKIN:	Just a harsh sharp shock,
SHEPPARD:	They won't want to do it again.
BOTH:	Lock me up it's a welcome break,
	When I decide I'll be back again.
	If a prison must be so harsh and cruel,
	A survivor must be invincible.
BLUESKIN:	What are we to do with Jonathan Wild?
SHEPPARD:	Sweep him under the carpet.
BLUESKIN:	Don't acknowledge his existence,
SHEPPARD:	It will only encourage him.
BLUESKIN:	Just another fence,
	We don't have to use him.
SHEPPARD:	Don't need to sell him goods,

BLUESKIN: (There's plenty of others),
SHEPPARD: Who'll pay better prices for the stuff.

BLUESKIN: There's no need to fear him,
SHEPPARD: He's not indestructible,
BLUESKIN: Many men have failed,
SHEPPARD: But we'll finish him off.

BOTH: Lock me up it's a welcome break,
When I decide I'll be back again.
If a prison must be so harsh and cruel,
A survivor must be invincible.

If a prison must be so harsh and cruel,
A survivor must be invincible.

SHEPPARD and BLUESKIN see the sign and exit.
JONATHAN WILD and FISTS step out from the shadows.

WILD: Well Mr. Fists, looks like the children need a little discipline. You do your best for them and this is how they treat you. No loyalty you see. I must be obeyed, not questioned - just like the King. *(To audience)* Keeping the status quo benefits everyone. *(To FISTS)* Find out who they use as a fence, then bring him to me.

Projection: **In a panic an orgy of selling stocks and shares began. By October 1720, porters and ladies maids (who had invested heavily) lost carriages and other luxuries they had bought. There were daily suicides, the Riot Act was read in Parliament. It was decided the National Debt would be split between the Treasury and the Bank of England.**

Scene Seventeen: Wild's office near the Old Bailey.

Caption: **17. Jack Sheppard's old benefactor, Mr. Kneebone, gives Wild the chance to take Sheppard and Blueskin.**

KNEEBONE sits at WILD's desk, WILD is reading his list. FISTS stands at the door, SMITH in the corner.

KNEEBONE: I think everything's there, seemed to know exactly what they wanted.

WILD: Lucky you weren't hurt Mr. Kneebone.

KNEEBONE: I suppose that's the way to look at it really.   No chance of getting anything back on the insurance: bubble company that didn't exist.

WILD: You try and make provisions for the future, but the government keep changing the rules.

KNEEBONE: Still, I understand Walpole's committed to low taxation, even cut land tax, that's some help.

WILD: For those of us who can afford to pay tax.

KNEEBONE: *(Standing to leave)* You won't catch me jumping off the monument Mr. Wild, even in a recession people need clothing.

WILD: Before you go Mr. Kneebone, does the name Jack Sheppard mean anything to you?

KNEEBONE: Of course, doubly so: I tried to set him up with a career, friend of mine Owen Wood, unfortunately he's gone now, as have many. And, as you know, Sheppard turned to crime; pity.

WILD: I think you should sit down.

KNEEBONE sits.

WILD: I have it on very strong authority that it was Jack Sheppard and an accomplice that turned over your house.

KNEEBONE: What?

WILD: I didn't mention it earlier, as prosecution depends on a key witness, but I have no doubt about his willingness to co-operate.

KNEEBONE: But I did so much for him?

WILD: The criminal has no scruples Mr. Kneebone. What I need to know is, would you testify?

KNEEBONE: Of course, but... I can't believe he could be guilty of such a thing?

WILD: Guilt is for the jury to decide, all I'm asking is that you identify him as his former benefactor. It may even be possible to retrieve some of your possessions.

KNEEBONE: Really?

WILD: Believe it or not Mr. Kneebone there are people in this City who buy goods, knowing them to be stolen. Without a thought of how they've been obtained.

KNEEBONE: Just name the date Mr. Wild, I'll be there.

KNEEBONE stands and shakes Wild's hand.

WILD: Thank you, good day.

FISTS shows KNEEBONE out, ROUSER and MOLLY drag in a chair with WILLIAM FIELD tied to it, gagged, he has obviously been roughed up.

FISTS: Do you want me to hit him again?

WILD: Not for the moment.   Take his gag off Moll.

MOLLY removes the gag.

MOLLY: There, see, my old man's not so bad.

WILD: As you probably heard Mr. Field the man that's just left was on the receiving end of your new clients' handy work.   While you were receiving his goods, he was receiving a great deal of grief, having worked all his life to accumulate the items taken in an afternoon.   And what for? So you could earn a few quid?   Sell a few things off cheap to your mates?

MOLLY: I don't suppose you thought you were taking much of a risk?

ROUSER: Don't suppose you thought the supplier mattered? As long as you got the goods.

WILD: But it does you see, because it affects people further up the chain: your gain is someone else's loss.   Probably wouldn't have occurred to you, if I hadn't got Mr. Fists to beat your face in? However, I am prepared to overlook this selfish streak.

MOLLY: That's nice isn't it?

SMITH takes a piece of paper over to FIELD.

WILD: I am inviting you to turn King's evidence, and shop Jack Sheppard and Joseph Black.   I've already got definite I.D.'s.

Pause.

FIELD: I ...can't.

MOLLY: Yes you can.   What you can't do is breath when your nose is crushed into your face.

- 77 -

FIELD: They'll kill me.

ROUSER: Mr. Wild wouldn't be that kind.

WILD: I'm offering you a golden opportunity Field.

> *There is a knock at the door. FIELD is gagged and dragged back out. FISTS opens the door. JOHN GAY enters.*

WILD: Yes sir?

GAY: Ah, erm I wonder if I could ask you for some help?

WILD: Come in, come in. Have you had something stolen?

GAY: Well, yes.

WILD: Give Mr. Smith your list and we'll see what we can do.

GAY: Erm, it's not that simple actually.

WILD: Oh?

GAY: Difficult to put a value on it you see. I'm a writer, John Gay *(Holding out his hand, which WILD ignores)*. Lost a manuscript, a new play, about a girl whose parents disapprove of her husband...

WILD: Seen it.

GAY: But you couldn't have...

WILD: Have you lost anything valuable or not?

GAY: It's priceless to me.

WILD: I've got a business to run here, highwaymen to get peached. Someone's probably nicked it for the string binding.

GAY: Do you have a daughter?

WILD glares at him.

GAY: Just curious.

FISTS starts to remove GAY.

GAY: What would you think if your daughter were to marry a highwayman?

GAY is thrown out of the door.

WILD: Writer's, biggest thieves of all. We'll probably see ourselves at the Goodman's Fields Theatre next. *(To audience)* Only I'll be Mr. Peachum and Sheppard'll be Captain MacHeath. *(To FISTS)* Go and persuade Field to sign that piece of paper.

Exit FISTS.

Darren Rapier

Scene Eighteen: Newgate Gaol.

Caption: **18. Wild has his throat cut from ear to ear.**

*SHEPPARD and BLUESKIN are in separate cells behind
bars. A GUARD sits outside, WILD and FISTS enter.*

WILD: Sheppard, Blueskin, how are you? Apart from
the impending hanging that is? Still, look on the
bright side, you could have been on your way to
America instead. Thought I conducted the
proceedings rather well, jury eating out of my
hand *(To audience)* As usual. *(To SHEPPARD
and BLUESKIN)* 'course wouldn't have secured it
without my old mate Field. You had a future
with me boys. *(Beat)* I've attended quite a few
hangings now, but I must say, this one really will
be a treat. Record turn out by the ladies for you
Jack, even if you would cut off their ring finger
as much as give them a peck on the cheek.
(To audience) I can see it now, sun blazing
down. Those two bundled into the cart, faces
pressed against the bars. Crack, the horses are
off with a jolt. The crowd lining the streets,
shouting "Thieves, murderers, burn in hell!",
fighting with the poor sods who admire you and
are hoping for a reprieve, so you can teach them
for being so stupid when you pick on them next
time. And above it all me, shouting: "My
children are coming!" Into Oxford Street, "My
children are coming!" The roads lined with
people, kids trying to keep up with the cart, to get
a last glimpse before they see them croak. "My
children are coming!" Into Tyburn Road, triple
tree in sight. Stands, packed with spectators,
wondering 'how will they die?' Bets taken on
whether they'll go out screaming like a baby.
Then all the tears, all the cries, all the ballads,
stop. And you'll swing, with your feet kicking at
the air, and your friends, if they can fight their
way through, will pull and pull until: Crack, it's
all over, bar the gibbets and the surgeons.

BLUESKIN: *(To audience)* Nice thought, but it wasn't to be.
               (To WILD) Jonathan.

WILD: Hmn.

               BLUESKIN indicates the GUARD.

WILD: Take a walk.   *(He tosses the GUARD some
               money).*

               The GUARD exits.

WILD: Well?

BLUESKIN: Something you might be interested in.

               *WILD walks over to the bars.   BLUESKIN indicates he
               wants him to come closer so SHEPPARD can't hear.
               WILD leans in.   BLUESKIN grabs him and pulls him to
               the bars, producing a knife he slits his throat.   WILD
               croaks loudly.   FISTS, grabbing the guards blanket,
               rushes over and hits BLUESKIN, throwing him back into
               the cell.   WILD falls to the floor, FISTS puts the blanket
               to WILD's throat which soon fills with blood.*

FISTS: Jonathan?   GUARD!!

BLUESKIN: Die you bastard!

FISTS: GUARD!!

SHEPPARD: Looks like you won't be making the trip after all.

FISTS: GUARD!!

               *A chord is struck.   WILD stands, his neck pouring with
               blood.*

BALLAD OF PITY.

WILD: Who do you pity?
               The man with his throat cut?

The man trying to help him?
The man who drew the knife?
The man who left his post?
The man who enjoys the deed?
Or the countless victims of them all?

Projection: **In 1721 Thomas Guy bought a plot of land, opposite the original site of St. Thomas's Hospital, to build Guy's Hospital. He had been a great benefactor to St. Thomas's, but felt it now catered too much for the rich.**

<u>Scene Nineteen:</u> Tyburn, 11th November 1724.

<u>Caption:</u> **19. The crowd gather to watch BLUESKIN's hanging.**

*The BALLAD SINGER sings to the crowd, which includes
the LANDLORD and FRIENDS, who try to ignore him
through fear of paying for the entertainment.
The gallows are in the distance, behind the audience.*

**BLUESKIN'S BALLAD
by Jonathan Swift, 1724.
(To the tune of Packington's Pound).**

SINGER: Ye fellows of Newgate whose Fingers are nice
In Diving in Pockets and Cogging of Dice;
Ye Sharpers so rich who can buy off the Noose,
Ye honest poor Rogues who Die in your shoes,
Attend and Draw near,
Good News you shall hear
How Honest *Wild's* Throat was cut Ear to Ear
Now *Blueskin's* sharp Penknife has set you at
Ease,
And ev'ry Man round me may rob if he please.

When to the Old Baily this *Blueskin* was led,
He held up his hand, his Indictment was read,
Loud rattled his Chain, near him honest *Wild*
stood,
For full Forty Pounds was the Price of his Blood.
Then Hopeless of Life
He drew his Penknife
And made a sad Widow of honest *Wild's* wife.
But forty Pounds paid her, her Grief shall
appease
And ev'ry Man round me may rob if he Please.

Some say there are Courtiers of highest Renown
Who steal the King's Gold and leave him but a
Crown;
Some say there are Peers and some Parliament
Men
Who meet once a Year to rob Courtiers again;

But let them have their Swing
To pillage the King,
And get a blue Ribbon instead of a string
For *Blueskin's* sharp Penknife has set you at
Ease,
And ev'ry Man round me may rob if he please.

Knaves of old to hide Guilt by their cunning
Inventions
Call Briberies Grants, and plain Robbery
Pensions.
Physicians and Lawyers who take their Degrees
To be learned Rouges, call their pilferings fees
Since this happy Day
Now ev'ry one may
Rob (as safe as in office) upon the High-way,
For *Blueskin's* sharp Penknife has set you at
Ease,
And ev'ry Man round me may rob if he please.

Some Rob in the *Customs*, some Cheat in the
'*xise*
But he who Robs *Both* is esteemed most wise
Church-Wardens who always have dreaded the
Halter
As yet only venture to steal from the Altar.
But now to get Gold
They may be more bold.
And rob on the High-way since honest *Wild's*
cold,
For *Blueskin's* sharp Penknife has set you at
Ease,
And ev'ry Man round me may rob if he please.

Some by *Publick Revenues* which pass thro' their
hands
Have purchas'd *Clean Houses* and bought *Dirty
Lands*;
Some to steal from a Charity think it No Sin
Which at home (says the proverb) does always
begin
If ever you be
Assign'd a Trustee

Treat not the Orphans like Masters in the
Chancery
For *Blueskin's* sharp Penknife has set you at
Ease,
And ev'ry Man round me may rob if he please.

What a Pother is here with *Woods* and his Brass
Who wou'd modestly make a few Half pennies
pass;
The Patent is good, and the Precident's old,
For *Diamede* changed his Copper for Gold;
But if *Ireland* despise
The new Half pennies
More safely to Rob on the Road I advise,
For *Blueskin's* sharp Penknife has set you at
Ease,
And ev'ry Man round me may rob if he please.

*The BALLAD SINGER holds out his hat but no one puts
money into it.   He exits.*

LANDLORD: *(Looking at his watch)* Soon time.

FRIEND 1:   How do you think he'll take it?

FRIEND 2:   He's an evil bastard.

FRIEND 3:   Must be hard, to do Wild in.

LANDLORD: He is not done in, he's merely resting.

FRIEND 2:   Pegged out last week I heard.

FRIEND 1:   His mate Rouser's declared himself King of
Southwark.

FRIEND 3:   There you go, Wild would have done him in by
now.

FRIEND 1:   Old Bailey's been quiet that's for sure.

LANDLORD: These things take time to heal.

FRIEND 2:   He had his throat cut clean through to his spine.

LANDLORD: Don't be ridiculous.

FRIEND 1:   Good job I say, might be safe to walk the streets at night.

LANDLORD: It's only Wild who's kept crime under control in the City. People like him arn't interested in harming the man in the street.

FRIEND 2:   That's true, apparently he used to send food round to those worse off than himself, can't be that bad.

FRIEND 1:   But who'd paid for it?

FRIEND 2:   Well he must have done.

LANDLORD: You're talking about a man who's had seventeen attempts on his life, who has a silver plate holding his head together.

FRIEND 2:   Did he?

LANDLORD: I hardly think a small penknife wound is going to harm him.

FRIEND 2:   Cutlass I heard.

LANDLORD: Oh shut up.

FRIEND 3:   Whether he's dead or not, I'll feel a lot safer in my bed when Blueskin, and Sheppard for that matter, have drawn their last breath.

FRIEND 1:   Did you ever meet them then?

FRIEND 3:   No, but my mates mate had a close call.

LANDLORD: I helped convict Sheppard you know.

FRIEND 1:   Why ain't they hanging them together?

LANDLORD: Twice the revenue I suppose: more here
              tomorrow for Sheppard.

FRIEND 2:   Makes you sick don't it, people haven't got
              anything better to do than gawp at some villain.

FRIEND 1:   Half these crooks only do it 'cause they want to
              get their faces seen at Tyburn.

FRIEND 2:   I don't know what's the matter with this country,
              lost our sense of pride since Queen Anne's gone.

FRIEND 1:   Queen Elizabeth, had something to be proud of
              then.

FRIEND 3:   Didn't have to worry about shutting your
              windows at night.

FRIEND 1:   He's on the gallows.

LANDLORD: Couple of minutes yet.

FRIEND 2:   Is he shaking?

FRIEND 1:   No, but he's putting up a fight.

LANDLORD: Why do they have to do that?   Why can't they
              just take it like a man?

FRIEND 3:   They're throwing mud at him now.

LANDLORD: No decency left.

FRIEND 1:   Where did you get that watch?

LANDLORD: Can't remember off hand.

FRIEND 2:   Here we go.

ALL: Oooo.

FRIEND 1:   Still kicking.

> *A PICKPOCKET walks past and bumps into the*
> *LANDLORD and takes his watch as:*

FRIEND 3:   Crowd's in the way now.

FRIEND 2:   Just see his head, still attached.

FRIEND 3:   I feel safer already.

LANDLORD: *(As the PICKPOCKET bumps into him)* Oi.

PICKPOCKET: *(Under breath)* Sorry mate.   *(Exits).*

LANDLORD: Hey!   My watch!

FRIEND 1:   Did he take your watch?

LANDLORD: Yes.

FRIEND 2:   Bloody liberty.

FRIEND 3:   You should have chased after him.

FRIEND 1:   Be long gone by now.

FRIEND 2:   Makes you sick doesn't it, all these people around
              and not one helping you.

FRIEND 1:   *(To audience)* Hanging is no deterrent to the man
              who doesn't think he'll be caught.

Scene Twenty: Newgate Gaol.

Caption: **20. Aided by Bess and Poll, Jack Sheppard escapes a second time from Newgate.**

BESS and POLL enter.   SHEPPARD is still behind bars, a GUARD sits outside his cell.

BESS: Oh Jack, can it really be you?

POLL: What has become of our poor lamb?

BESS: We miss you down at the convent.

POLL: Could it be that one so dear has been the victim of so cruel a fate?

They throw themselves at the foot of the bars and weep melodramatically.   BESS drops a file loudly to the floor. The GUARD looks up, they turn, stand and face him.

POLL: Oh how could you be so heartless?

BESS: To deprive those tiny children of the only joy they have.   *(She kicks the file to SHEPPARD).*

POLL: To take the finest tenor from our choir.

GUARD: I'm just trying to do a job ladies.

BESS: He's right Poll, it's just a job.   If he wasn't doing it, someone else would be.   We must remember that, unlike ourselves, some people never obtain satisfaction in their work.

POLL: Would you be so kind as to get us some wine?

GUARD: Can't do that madam, I'm not at liberty to leave the room.

Darren Rapier

BESS:	(Moving over to him and taking his attention away from the cell) I admire a man with a sense of duty.
GUARD:	Do you madam?
BESS:	Yes, I think that's why I went into the church.

Behind them SHEPPARD, helped by POLL, is franticly filing at the bars on the wicket.

GUARD:	I must say, you don't look like a nun.
BESS:	That's the whole point of our order, to blend in: Free the soul, trapped by society.
GUARD:	Oh.

He turns to POLL. SHEPPARD turns away abruptly.

GUARD:	Are you from the same order?
POLL:	Yes, orthodox radicals.
BESS:	Is there a lot of training for your job?

The GUARD turns back to BESS. SHEPPARD continues filing.

GUARD:	No not really.
BESS:	Do you think I could do it?
GUARD:	A woman?
BESS:	I suppose not. You have to be a certain type of person.
GUARD:	That's right. Not anyone could stick around here all day.
BESS:	(To audience) Fewer than he anticipates.

GUARD: Vigilance, that's the main part of the job.

SHEPPARD climbs over the wicket.

BESS: I bet you have to be fit though don't you?

GUARD: Oh, yes, yes.

BESS: And intelligent?

GUARD: Well...

BESS: I could tell. You look like an intelligent sort of man, alert, fit.

The GUARD is about to turn again when:

BESS: Are you doing anything tomorrow night?

GUARD: Er.

BESS: It's my night off you see, thought you might like to do something?

GUARD: I didn't realise you had nights off?

BESS: Not normally, normally we work flat out.

GUARD: I should be free tomorrow, as long as the hanging goes alright. *(Fancying his chances)* What did you have in mind?

SHEPPARD and POLL sneak out behind him.

BESS: Oh... I'll surprise you.

BESS slowly backs out of the door, the GUARD follows her smiling, she stops him at the door and blows him a kiss. BESS exits. The GUARD, pleased with himself, turns towards the cell to gloat. Suddenly he realises it is empty.

Darren Rapier

GUARD: Bollocks!

Snap to song lighting.

BALLAD OF RETRIBUTION (reprise).

BALLAD SINGER steps forward.

SINGER: Don't think you've got away,
                Just because nothing's happened today,
                You'll be caught out,
                No doubt about-
                That,
                Is there?

                Good deeds don't go unnoticed,
                Help others you'll be rewarded,
                Won't you?
                See it in life,
                Don't you?

                Don't you?

                Sheppard couldn't stay away,
                Went to the country,
                But back within days.
                Re-captured in Finchley,
                To Newgate and soon he,
                Was manacled and chained,
                To the floor.

Scene Twenty-one: Newgate Gaol.

Caption: **21. With the aid of a crooked nail Sheppard escapes from Newgate for the last time.**

The GUARD leaves the cell laughing.

GUARD: Get out of that. Ha, ha.

The GUARD exits. SHEPPARD looks round.

SHEPPARD: *(To musicians).* Two, three, four.

*To gentle musical accompaniment SHEPPARD mimes his escape, as if performing an escapologist's act. He takes the nail and uses it to release the lock on his chains. He slips off the chains and puts the nail obviously into his pocket. BESS appears with a cardboard 'flue' shaped object that says '**CHIMNE**'. She displays this (like a magician's assistant). SHEPPARD mimes taking an iron bar out of the chimney and climbing up it. POLL appears with a sign saying '**THE RED ROOM**'. SHEPPARD looks round and sees a door (a cardboard one that BESS is holding, with a sign on it saying '**UNOPENED FOR SEVEN YEAR**'). SHEPPARD removes the sign and starts work on the lock with the nail. He opens it in seconds. SHEPPARD mimes a wall, then mimes breaking through it. POLL now holds a sign saying '**THE CHAPEL**'. SHEPPARD looks left and right and exits briskly. The musicians play a 'Ta Da'. SHEPPARD takes a bow.*

Scene Twenty-two: The Streets around Newgate.

Caption: **22. Jack Sheppard celebrates his escape and is re-**
            captured.

SHEPPARD, BESS and POLL stagger through the streets
singing. POLL and BESS try to keep SHEPPARD form
being too loud.

BALLAD OF INVINCIBILITY (2nd reprise).

SHEPPARD/POLL/ BESS:

What are we to do with undesirables?
Sweep them under the carpet?
Don't acknowledge their existence,
It will encourage others.

Get them off the streets?
We don't want to see them.
Don't write about them,
(Well just a little),
Merely to show how bad they are.

We don't need to teach them,
Show them alternatives,
Just a harsh sharp shock,
They won't want to do it again.

Lock me up it's a welcome break,
When I decide I'll be back again.
If a prison must be so harsh and cruel,
A survivor must be invincible.

Some CONSTABLES appear in the background.

SHEPPARD: Lock me up it's a welcome break,
              When I decide I'll be back again.

The two women are grabbed from behind and taken off.

SHEPPARD: If a prison must be so harsh and cruel,
              A survivor must be invincible.

If a prison must be so harsh and cruel,
A survivor must be invincible.

SHEPPARD turns to see the CONSTABLES.

SHEPPARD: Bollocks!

He is too drunk to resist and they take him away.

Scene Twenty-three: Wild's office near the Old Bailey.

Caption: **23. Having survived the attack by Blueskin, Wild feels vulnerable to the increasing interest of the authorities.**

WILD sits, his neck in thick blood stained bandages, MOLLY sits beside him. FISTS stands by the door and SMITH in the corner. The EARL of DARTMOUTH stands centre stage.

MOLLY: What my husband's trying to say is: These magistrates have got a bloody liberty. The amount of villains he's brought in, they should give him the freedom of the City, not try and trip him up every five minutes. What with him being so poorly as well.

EARL: I quite understand Mrs. Wild, but there's little I can do.

MOLLY: Surely you must have some influence, what's the point of being an Earl?

EARL: The public has lost it's faith in the legal system, the fact that Jonathan was instrumental in the capture of two notorious villains hasn't helped. If everyone thought they could make a better job of implementing the law than the authorities, who knows where it might end?

MOLLY: But they wanted them caught.

EARL: Only to prove they hadn't lost control. The public only wanted them caught while they felt personally threatened. The thought of 'it could be me next time'. People forget. Sheppard is 'the man who's escaped from Newgate three times, beaten the system', not 'the man who beats his victims for financial gain'. *(Looks to audience)* ask them.

MOLLY: There are hundreds of other people they could pick on, why us? I can honestly say we have never personally stolen a single item.

EARL: Jonathan has elevated himself to the position of a successful self made man. If it can be proved he got there immorally everyone is satisfied: The Government have found a scapegoat on who they can pin 'London's Decline', asserting the fact 'true gain is only possible through hard work'; The authorities have brought in a 'major figure'; The Church can claim 'divine retribution'; The papers have a 'story' to tell and the public can enjoy seeing someone better off than themselves suffering: works every time. Heaven knows how many times I've been accused of 'deserving it' when the roof of my carriage is slashed open. I'm afraid all you can do is hope they find someone else to pick on before you get caught out; apparently Fielding is already sighting foreigners as a cause for concern.

MOLLY: Well, thank you for calling, it's been most helpful.

EARL: Not at all, good to see you're up and well Jonathan.

WILD nods.

EARL: Oh, there was one other thing. I wonder if you might be able to get me some cheap lace? Let me know - who can say I may think of someone I could speak to?

MOLLY looks at WILD who nods. The EARL turns to leave, FISTS opens the door but the LANDLORD rushes in bumping into the EARL, who remains as:

LANDLORD: Oh pardon me. Mr. Wild, I knew you'd be open for business as usual.

WILD nods.

LANDLORD: That watch of mine, can you believe it?

WILD signals to SMITH to fetch the watch, SMITH exits.

LANDLORD: No point in having anything decent if you have to keep it locked up.

EARL: I quite agree. One should be able to use things without fear of undesirables taking a fancy to them.

LANDLORD: Too right.

SMITH enters with the watch and hands it to the LANDLORD.

LANDLORD: *(Showing the watch to the EARL).*   A timepiece is made to be used, not envied or worn as a statement of affluence.

EARL: Just a minute! This is my watch!! It was taken from my house, bloody near wrecked the place.

MOLLY: Yours?

LANDLORD: I beg your pardon, I bought that watch in good faith.

EARL: It's got my initials on the back.

MOLLY: There must be some mistake?

EARL: There is no mistake. *(To LANDLORD)* How could you afford a fifty guinea watch?

WILD: *(Croaks)* Fifty?

MOLLY: Alright dear. *(Then to EARL)* I assure you we had no idea the watch was stolen.

LANDLORD: That cost me a pint of my best ale.

EARL: Here's a shilling for your ale sir, *(tossing the money on the floor and grabbing the watch)* how dare you devalue such an item.   No wonder these rogues persist in plaguing our City, with people like you prepared to fund their enterprise.

LANDLORD: I merely wanted a nice watch.

EARL: Exactly sir.   Good day.

The EARL leaves.   WILD shakes his head in despair.   He beckons MOLLY and whispers to her.

MOLLY: Mr. Smith, Jonathan would like you to contact our suppliers with regard to the Earl's lace.

SMITH: Certainly.

SMITH exits.

MOLLY: Well, I can only hope that we make amends with the gentleman, *(looks at LANDLORD)* for all our sakes.

LANDLORD: I only wanted my watch back.   He can bloody well afford it anyway.

MOLLY: No doubt there are a lot of rumours in the City as regards my husband's health?

LANDLORD: A few people have remarked on it.

MOLLY: Well, as you can see, he's fully recovered.   No cause for concern: business as usual.   I'm sure your customers would be very pleased to hear that.   *(The LANDLORD is puzzled).*   You've been there quite a while now, regular clientele, miss the old place if something happened I expect?

The penny drops.

LANDLORD: Oh, yeah.

MOLLY: Now would you like to see a selection of our
              watches?   We'll do a special price for you.

Scene Twenty-four: Newgate Gaol.

<u>Caption:</u> **24. Jack Sheppard receives his well wishers before he is hanged.**

> *SHEPPARD sits, held by special irons.   He is surrounded by people including the ORDINARY and Sir JAMES THORNHILL (who is painting him) as well as various MEN and WOMEN.   The GUARD is pushed to one corner.   The ORDINARY is offering him a bible.*

SHEPPARD: ...in my situation a file would be worth all the bibles in the world.

> *The VISITOR's laugh.   The ORDINARY retracts the offer.*

THORNHILL: I must say Jack it's a damn shame they're hanging you.   With your wit and intelligence you could have gone into politics.

SHEPPARD: They haven't hung me yet James.   How's the portrait coming?

THORNHILL: Fine.

WOMAN: Is it true Sir James that you nearly lost your life while painting the ceiling at St. Pauls?

THORNHILL: Quite a close call yes, nearly stepped backwards off the scaffold. Luckily my assistant had the sense to smear the paintwork, causing me to rush forward and stop him.   If he'd have shouted instead I might not be here today.

ORDINARY: The Lord moves in mysterious ways.

SHEPPARD: I must have a look at your ceiling when I get out.

THORNHILL: Still optimistic Jack?

SHEPPARD: Invincible, that's me.

WOMAN: I've written to the King, requesting a reprieve.

ORDINARY: On what grounds?

WOMAN: On the grounds that I have been here every day
            this week, and Mr. Sheppard has not shown the
            slightest hint of incivility.

SHEPPARD: Thanks, maybe I'll pay you a visit as well?

WOMAN: My door will always be open.

SHEPPARD: No need to worry about that.

> *The WOMAN giggles.*

ORDINARY: Don't you ever stop to think your talents could
            have been put to better use?

SHEPPARD: Whose use? You're getting your account of my
            'life' to sell at the hanging aren't you? Not that
            you'll be able to sell it incomplete. I've used my
            talents to give people what they want: a hero.

ORDINARY: Heroes do good Mr.Sheppard.

SHEPPARD: Do they? Only if you're on their side, surely?
            Look at Marlborough, those people are heroes to
            us, murderers to others. You have to put the
            suffering out of your mind, if you want to enjoy
            the benefits. Just a question of perspective; Sir
            James knows all about perspective, don't you
            James?

THORNHILL: Eh... oh absolutely. Very important.

SHEPPARD: Don't forget, I've done what no one has ever done
            before; I'm the man who's escaped from Newgate
            - three times.

> *Snap to song lighting. Behind the BALLAD SINGER, as
> he sings, a screen is brought forward a sign says
> 'TYBURN, 16th November 1724' and the hanging at*

Tyburn is projected onto it. At first we see the scaffold (triple tree). As the song progresses we see SHEPPARD's silhouette go through the motions of a hanging, ending with the body swinging on the rope.

Darren Rapier

BALLAD OF A LUCKY MAN.

SINGER: Escaped from Newgate three times,
Surely a feat to admire?
But what of the numerous crimes?
A detail the public don't require.

On the day of execution,
The Gaoler searched his clothes,
And badly cut his hand on,
A penknife there enclosed.
Two thousand turned out,
For the Paddington Fair,
Bets placed on the doubt,
That he'd end his life there.

Escaped from Newgate three times,
Surely a feat to admire?
But what of the numerous crimes?
A detail the public don't require.

As the cart drew away,
And his weight closed the noose,
Friends tried to reach him,
To cut Sheppard loose.
Well wishing admirers,
Who thought they'd be smart,
Feared dissection by surgeons,
And ripped him apart.

Escaped from Newgate three times,
Surely a feat to admire?
But what of the numerous crimes?
A detail the public don't require.

Tell us how dashing and daring,
But spare us the victim's report,
Their wining voice has no bearing,
On our romantic view of this sort.

Escaped from Newgate three times,
Surely a feat to admire?
But what of the numerous crimes?

A detail the public don't require.

(Spoken to audience)
There is no last minute reprieve.

Scene Twenty-Five: The Old Bailey's Justice Hall.

Caption **25. Jonathan Wild is sentenced to death for**
'Receiving' £40 worth of stolen lace and selling
them back to the original owner.

WILD stands in the dock, still in bandages, throughout the
scene his voice gets worse. MOLLY stands beside him.
TOFF is his defence lawyer. Also present are: The
JUDGE, JURY, COUNSEL for the king, FISTS etc. and
the CLERK.

CLERK: Mr. Jonathan Wild you are charged with:
                Stealing fifty yards of lace, valued at £40,
                receiving the same and selling them back to the
                original owner, without discovering or
                apprehending, or causing to be apprehended and
                brought to justice, the persons that committed the
                said felony.   How do you plead?

WILD: *(Gruffly and quietly)* Not guilty.

MOLLY: *(Very loudly)* Not guilty.

The CLERK sits and the COUNSEL stands.

COUNSEL: Counsel for the King would like to call Mrs.
                Sarah Jackson to the stand.

Mrs. JACKSON takes the oath.

JACKSON: I Sarah Jackson do solemnly swear to tell the
                truth, the whole truth and nothing but the truth,
                so help me God.

COUNSEL: You are Mrs. Sarah Jackson, of Tothill Fields?

JACKSON: Yes.

TOFF: Objection.   The Counsel is leading the witness.

WILD: Shut up Toff.

JUDGE: Overruled.

COUNSEL: What is the livelihood of you and your Husband?

JACKSON: We import and sell needle-point lace.

COUNSEL: Would you kindly tell the court of the events which took place on the night of February the Twenty-second of this year, Seventeen Twenty-Five?

JACKSON: I was at home with my husband... *(She bursts into tears)*.

TOFF: Objection. Witness trying to gain the sympathy of the Jury.

COUNSEL: Where is your husband Mrs. Jackson?

JACKSON: St. Thomas's Hospital, recovering from wounds inflicted that night.

JUDGE: Objection overruled.

COUNSEL: If you would please tell the court the events of that night?

JACKSON: About nine O'clock we retired. Later that evening, probably two hours or so, we heard noises downstairs in the shop. My husband went to investigate and there discovered a man passing our goods through the window to an accomplice. My husband challenged him and the man fled.

COUNSEL: Did you're husband try to pursue the man?

JACKSON: Yes. He chased him towards Peter Street and there... there the two men set about him and left him for dead.

COUNSEL: Thank you Mrs. Jackson, I'll try to be brief.
            What exactly was taken from your premises the
            night of your husband's assault?

TOFF: Objection.   The assault is surely irrelevant, it is
            the alleged theft that is in question?

JUDGE: Sustained.   Please re-phrase the question.

COUNSEL: Could you please tell the court what was stolen
            that night?

JACKSON: Fifty yards of lace, amounting to Forty pounds in
            value.

COUNSEL: *(Showing her the lace).*   Is this that same lace?

JACKSON: Yes.

COUNSEL: Exhibit 'A' your honour.

The lace is shown to the JUDGE and JURY.

JUDGE: Very nice.   Forty you say?   Do you give
            Judiciary discounts?

COUNSEL looks at the JUDGE disdainfully.

JUDGE: Never mind, I'll speak with you later.

COUNSEL: Mrs. Jackson, did you attempt to recover the
            lace?

JACKSON: Yes.

COUNSEL: How did you go about this?

JACKSON: By visiting Mr. Wild's Enquiry office.

COUNSEL: And what was the result?

JACKSON: A few days after informing Mr. Wild I returned
            to his office and was told I should go to a certain

place, at a certain time, where I may have my goods returned: for the sum of twenty pounds, 'no questions asked'.

COUNSEL: Do you see Mr. Wild in court this morning?

JACKSON: Yes.

COUNSEL: Would you point him out to us please?

JACKSON points to WILD.

WILD: *(To Audience, with normal voice)* You try to help someone...

COUNSEL: Am I to take it therefore that Mr. Wild offered no explanation, as to his acquisition of the said lace?

JACKSON: That is correct.

COUNSEL: And what happened when you went to obtain your goods?

JACKSON: Following the advice of Mr. Pargiter...

WILD: *(Gruffly)* Bastard.

Most have not fully caught the outburst but MOLLY calms WILD.

JACKSON: Following the advice of Mr. Pargiter I took a constable with me. When we arrived at Field Lane, as requested, a man approached me and asked for the money. On a pre-arranged signal the Constable revealed himself and the man was arrested.

COUNSEL: Thank you Mrs. Jackson.

JUDGE: *(Looking at Toff).* Do you have any questions for this witness?

TOFF:
Yes your honour. Mrs. Jackson you say your husband currently resides at St. Thomas's? A worthy institution, paid for by private funds.

JACKSON:
Yes?

TOFF:
From the funds of 'individuals'. You also say your husband's injury was caused when he pursued the alleged thieves? A courageous act of 'individual' law enforcement?

JACKSON:
Well no...

TOFF:
And yet, my client stands in the dock for exactly such acts of personal valour? For 'caring for others', as that noble institution does, for upholding the law, as your husband tried to do. Such is his commitment to society?

COUNSEL:
Objection. The building of a hospital will benefit the whole community, of future generations, the running of which cannot be compared to that of a business. *(Pause as the entire cast look at the audience)* Can it? *(unsure, they look back)* As for defending one's property, it's no more than any other man would do.

TOFF:
No more, precisely. Where as Mr. Wild goes further, he tries to protect that of others.

JUDGE:
What exactly was the objection?

TOFF:
That definition is dependant on perspective.

COUNSEL:
That you cannot compare the business activities of Mr. Wild, to those of someone trying to help people or enforce the law.

JUDGE:
Erm. Sustained, due to the fact that I would not like to upset Mrs. Jackson. *(He smiles at her).*

TOFF: Very well. Why did you go to my client's office
            Mrs. Jackson?

JACKSON: For help.

TOFF: Where you charged anything?

JACKSON: No.

TOFF: So am I to take it that Mr. Wild made enquiries
            for you free of charge?

JACKSON: Yes but...

TOFF: And by making those enquiries obtained the
            goods you had asked him to?

JACKSON: Yes but...

TOFF: Would you rather the goods remained lost?

JACKSON: No.

TOFF: Then it seems my client merely did as you
            requested. He gave you all you asked for?

JACKSON: But he failed to tell me his supplier.

TOFF: Is this usual?

JACKSON: I beg your pardon?

TOFF: Is it usual? In business; to disclose your
            supplier? If I asked you the exact address of
            your supplier of lace for instance?

JACKSON: Well no but...

TOFF: Then how am I to know? If I wanted to make
            sure that the lace maker was a good honest
            fellow? That they were paid a decent wage?

That their craft was not devalued by those eager to make a swift profit?

JACKSON: Surely your concern would be the quality of the product you were buying?

TOFF: And the price, but little else. Mr. Wild stands before you, the victim of his efforts to bring people to justice. Can you blame him for not asking too many questions about your precious lace?

JACKSON: My husband lies in hospital.

TOFF: I'm afraid you cannot accuse a man, in my client's current state of health, of being capable of affecting that of your husband's? Mr. Wild is in no fit state to be running around the streets of London for a few yards of lace. That concludes my questioning.

Mrs. JACKSON steps down.

CLERK: Call Mr. Isaac Harvey.

WILD: Isaac Harvey?

Enter ROUSER. There is much commotion.

FISTS: Rouser! I'll have you!

JUDGE: Order.

SMITH: You weasel!

JUDGE: Order! Do I have to clear the courtroom?

ROUSER takes the oath.

ROUSER: I, Isaac Harvey, do solemnly swear to tell the truth, the whole truth and nothing but the truth, so help me God.

FISTS: God won't help you!

COUNSEL: Mr. Harvey, I understand you worked with Mr. Wild?

ROUSER: A while ago, yes.

COUNSEL: Could you tell us how you first came to know the gentleman?

ROUSER: I first met Mr. Wild in the Poultry Compter, where he was being held on account of debt.

TOFF: Objection.   Irrelevant.

JUDGE: Overruled.

ROUSER: Where he was imprisoned for debt.

COUNSEL: And when did you next see Mr. Wild?

ROUSER: About two years later.

COUNSEL: In what circumstances?

ROUSER: Very different, he seemed quite the gentleman.

COUNSEL: You say 'seemed'.

ROUSER: Compared to how he was before, rough, violent...

WILD: I have never been violent you bastard!

WILD tries to clamber over the bar to get to ROUSER. MOLLY and the OFFICIALS, helped by TOFF, prevent him.

JUDGE: Mr. Wild, would you like me to send you back to the cells?

TOFF: My client is a little distressed to see someone on whom he has bestowed so much friendship, lying so viciously.

JUDGE: May I remind you that the agreement to turn King's Evidence is not viewed lightly. It is not Mr. Harvey that is on trial here. Continue.

COUNSEL: What was the result of meeting Mr. Wild?

ROUSER: He offered me a position in his firm.

COUNSEL: And did you accept?

ROUSER: What with jobs being scarce and my age getting on it seemed like I had no choice.

COUNSEL: We quite understand Mr. Harvey, did you take the job?

ROUSER: Yes.

COUNSEL: And what did you find out about Mr. Wild's 'firm'?

ROUSER: It soon became apparent that the office of Mr. Wild was frequented by a number of highwaymen, pick-pockets, housebreakers and the like.

COUNSEL: That did not seem to be under arrest you mean?

TOFF: Objection: leading question.

JUDGE: Overruled.

ROUSER: No sir, not under arrest, confederates.

There is a melodramatic gasp from those assembled.

COUNSEL: Are we to take it that Mr. Wild knowingly associated with felons?

ROUSER: Yes. Jack Sheppard, Joseph Black, even Mr.
             Hitchin, the late City Marshal.

JUDGE: Do we have any of these people present today?

COUNSEL: No sir, they've all been hanged.

JUDGE: Jolly good, ruffians.

ROUSER: Further more, he ordered them to rob people.

TOFF: Objection.

ROUSER: Then sold the booty back to the owners.

TOFF: Objection!

The courtroom erupts as...

ROUSER: And what he   FISTS: Shut it!
couldn't sell back at   TOFF: Objection!
the right price, he sold   WILD: You're dead!
at market or broke up for JUDGE: Order!
export or had melted down TOFF: Objection!
and re-sold!   JUDGE: Order!

Blackout.

Fade up: Later that day, positions have changed.
COUNSEL has a black eye, the JUDGE's wig is in
disarray, clothes are torn, ROUSER has gone, the public
gallery is empty.
WILD stands at the bar.

COUNSEL: Members of the jury I put it to you that for many
             years past Mr. Jonathan Wild has been the
             confederate with great numbers of highwaymen,
             pick-pockets, housebreakers, shop-lifters and
             other thieves.
             That he has formed a kind of corporation of
             thieves, of which he is head and director, and that
             notwithstanding his pretended services, in

detecting and prosecuting offenders, he procures such only to be hanged as conceal their booty, or refuse to share it with him.

That he has divided the town and country into so many districts, and appointed distinct gangs for each, who regularly account with him of their robberies.   That he has also a particular set to steal at churches in time of divine service: and likewise other moving detachments to attend at court, on birth-days, balls etc. and at both houses of parliament, circuits and country fairs.

That the persons employed by him are for the most part felons convict, who have returned from transportation before the time, for which they are transported, is expired; and that he makes choice of them to be his agents, because they cannot be legal evidences against him, and because he has it in his power to take from them what part of the stolen goods he thinks fit, and otherwise use them ill, or hang them as he pleases.

That he has from time to time supplied such convicted felons with money and clothes, and lodged them in his own house, the better to conceal them: particularly some, against whom there are now informations for counterfeiting and diminishing broad pieces and guineas.

That he has not only been a receiver of stolen goods, as well as of writings of all kinds, for near fifteen years past, but has frequently been a confederate, and robbed along with the previously mentioned convicted felons.

That, in order to carry on these vile practices, to gain some credit with the ignorant multitude, he usually carries a short silver staff, as a badge of authority from the government, which he produces, when he himself is concerned with robbing.

That he has, under his care and direction, several warehouses for receiving and concealing stolen goods; and also a ship for carrying off jewels, watches, and other valuable goods, to Holland, where he has a superannuated thief for his factor.

That he keeps in pay several artists to make alterations, and transform watches, seals, snuff-boxes, rings and other valuable things, that they might not be known, several of which he used to present to such persons as he thought might be of service to him.

That he seldom or never helps the owners to the notes and papers they have lost, unless he finds them able exactly to specify and describe them, and then often insists on more than half the value.

And lastly, it appears that he has often sold human blood, by procuring false evidence to swear persons into facts they were not guilty of; sometimes to prevent them from being evidences against himself, and at other times for the sake of the great reward given by the government.

To conclude: I therefore feel it is your duty to find Jonathan Wild guilty on both counts.

The COUNSEL returns to his chair. TOFF stands.

TOFF: Ladies and gentlemen of the jury. You must ask yourselves: What has Jonathan Wild done that is so wrong?

COUNSEL: Ha.

WILD groans in the background, feeling this line of approach may be fruitless. Throughout the following speech the JURY gets more and more emotional and end in tears. WILD looks more feeble and harmless as TOFF proceeds.

TOFF: He has merely tried to give people what they wanted. He has been many times in this court, standing in the shoes of my learned friend: one hundred felons sent to the gallows. But you say: 'Were they guilty?' Of course. Maybe not, as my learned friend says, 'as charged' but guilty none the less, by jury defined: All thieves.

My client has steadily built up a business from nothing. He came to our great City to find his fortune, but instead found only injustice. Not allowing this to affect his optimism he continued to struggle on. Soon he had managed to earn enough to buy a modest home, some would be happy with that, not Mr. Wild. He knew the people of London needed him. He saw people's homes and livelihoods ruined, he saw their most treasured possessions being sold the next day for a song. He knew something must be done to control this sorry state of affairs. Charging a meagre fee for his services he set up business. Even when the authorities took away that small income Jonathan Wild continued, he knew people still wanted his service. His business has survived the rigours of the collapse of the South Sea Bubble. He has continued regardless of numerous threats on his life. And what do we offer him? *(He looks over at the forlorn Wild)* Standing before you is a broken man; a man disillusioned with all his country has promised him: Wealth, Stability, Justice.

To find my client guilty of theft, would surely be to sentence us all. If guilt is to be defined as 'not asking too many questions' who is without it? 'Never look a gift horse in the mouth.' Not a care for its breeding? Nor stables? Nor acquisition? As long as we benefit by the gift. And the argument is the same, be it horses, food, luxuries, taxes: Ask not from where it comes, merely how much. To sentence Jonathan Wild to death for theft, would be to say that anyone who buys underpriced goods without asking questions is as bad as the thief. Surely not so: Is it they who sneak around in the dead of night, they who inflict pain and suffering on the former owners of the items, no. They merely get a good deal, and where is the harm in that?

JUDGE: *(Also tearful)* Members of the Jury I must ask you to consider the two arguments put before you well, before reaching your verdict.

The JURY confer in whispers some still sniffing. The
HEAD JUROR looks at the JUDGE.

JUROR: Your honour, we have considered the evidence
              before us and certainly cannot find the defendant
              guilty of theft.

WILD and TOFF look at each other and smile.

JUROR: However, on the count of trying to make money
              by selling lace back to the original owner -
              something we would never have dreamed of
              doing - we find this despicable and our verdict is
              guilty as charged.

WILD: What!

WILD leaps over the bar and grabs the JUROR by the
throat. Several people try to pull him off.

MOLLY: Jonathan your neck.

JUDGE: *(Calmly)* Jonathan Wild, I sentence you to be
              hanged at Tyburn and then gibbeted, that'll teach
              you.

WILD is dragged out as:

THIEVES: *(Off)* Our Father's coming to Tyburn!

WILD: I'll kill you Toff!

THIEVES: *(Off)* Our Father's coming to Tyburn!

TOFF: I'm sorry.

THIEVES: *(Off)* Our Father's coming to Tyburn!

MOLLY: Sorry ain't good enough.

THIEVES: *(Off)* Our Father's coming to Tyburn!

Darren Rapier

JUDGE:	Perhaps a short spot of chocolate before the next case?
THIEVES:	*(Off)* Our Father's coming to Tyburn!
TOFF:	Jonathan please.
THIEVES:	*(Off)* Our Father's coming to Tyburn!
WILD:	I'll get out, I'll kill the lot of you!

The proceedings gradually dissolve as people leave. The BALLAD SINGER steps forward and speaks to the audience.

SINGER: With the death of Jonathan Wild the streets of London ran riot. Every villain was out for himself, in parliament Walpole exclaimed "...one is forced to travel, even at noon as if one was going into battle."
I wonder, are these the 'Old Values' we should be getting back to? Or should we perhaps endeavour to find new ones?

BALLAD OF PITY (reprise).

Who do you pity?
Those who get what they deserve?
Those who profit out of others?
Those who offer costly comforts?
Those who sell out their colleagues?
Those who justify their actions?
Or the man, hanged in Seventeen Twenty-five?

THE END

© Darren Rapier 14th February 2009

The Thieftaker

Darren Rapier

Other Plays by the same author include:

PEOPLE IN GLASS HOUSES

SMOKE

BOOM

EXTENSIONS OF LOVE

THE SNOW QUEEN

WORLDS APART

THE LITTLE MERMAID

1001 ARABIAN NIGHTS

CLARA AND THE NUTCRACKER

www.darrenrapier.co.uk

DARREN RAPIER

Darren Rapier trained at Rose Bruford College, graduating in 1995 with a degree in writing. He has written for film, television and theatre. Plays include *The Thieftaker,* about the first real gangster in early Eighteenth Century London; *People in Glass Houses*, a futuristic absurd comedy; *Smoke*, a play with music, about the railway 'improvements' and clearances of 1863; *Boom*, a community play set in 1936, about the housing boom in the South East; *Extensions of Love*, about one woman's obsession with another and *Worlds Apart*, set in India and the UK. Adaptations for children have included *The Snow Queen, The Little Mermaid, 1001 Arabian Nights* and *Clara and the Nutcracker.* Short plays include *The Gallery,* and the ten minute musical *Dying for a Kipp* at Greenwich Theatre. In 2007 he wrote and co-directed *Payback* for Greenwich and Lewisham Young Peoples' Theatre and *Departures* for the National Youth Theatre. He has written and directed two short films *It Is* and *The Race,* is a writer on *Doctors* for the BBC and has two feature films in development. Darren has been short listed for the Carl Forman Award at BAFTA, is a selected short film writer for TAPS and was a finalists in the BBC Talent Television Drama initiative in 2002. His radio play *Vital Statistics* was part of BBC Radio Drama/Hampstead Theatre's 'Stages of Sound' 2006. Darren is also Artistic Director of *Spanner in the Works,* who run drama based workshops in schools, hospitals and museums and a freelance drama trainer and facilitator.